Curse of the *Arctic Star*

Nancy Drew DIARIES™

Curse of the *Arctic Star*

#1

CAROLYN KEENE

Aladdin

NEW YORK LONDON TORONTO SYDNEY NEW DELHI

This book is a work of fiction. Any references to historical events, real people,
or real places are used fictitiously. Other names, characters, places, and events are products of the
author's imagination, and any resemblance to actual events or places or persons,
living or dead, is entirely coincidental.

ALADDIN

An imprint of Simon & Schuster Children's Publishing Division

1230 Avenue of the Americas, New York, NY 10020

First Aladdin paperback edition February 2013

Copyright © 2013 by Simon & Schuster

All rights reserved, including the right of reproduction in whole or in part in any form.

ALADDIN is a trademark of Simon & Schuster, Inc., and related logo
is a registered trademark of Simon & Schuster, Inc.

NANCY DREW, NANCY DREW DIARIES, and related logo are trademarks of
Simon & Schuster, Inc.

Also available in an Aladdin hardcover edition.

For information about special discounts for bulk purchases, please contact
Simon & Schuster Special Sales at 1-866-506-1949 or business@simonandschuster.com.

The Simon & Schuster Speakers Bureau can bring authors to your live event.
For more information or to book an event contact the Simon & Schuster Speakers Bureau
at 1-866-248-3049 or visit our website at www.simonspeakers.com.

Designed by Karina Granda

The text of this book was set in Adobe Caslon Pro.

Manufactured in the United States of America 0719 OFF

20

Library of Congress Control Number 2012949338

ISBN 978-1-4169-9072-7 (pbk)

ISBN 978-1-4424-6610-4 (hc)

ISBN 978-1-4424-5162-9 (eBook)

Contents

Dear Diary,

I DIDN'T ACTUALLY BELIEVE THAT A luxurious cruise ship could have any _real_ mysteries onboard.

Boy, was I wrong!

The minute we set sail, we were in mysteries up to our ears. I don't think I'll have any time to enjoy Alaska, and I've always wanted to visit the Last Frontier and pan for gold or even go dog sledding. . . .

Gotta go—George just yelled my name!

It's always something!

CHAPTER ONE

Bon Voyage

"NAME AND CABIN NUMBER, PLEASE?" THE efficient-looking porter asked, reaching for the large green suitcase sitting on the dock beside me.

"Nancy Drew. Hollywood Suite." I shrugged and shot a glance at my two best friends. "That's all they told us—I don't know the number."

The porter smiled. He was a short, muscular man dressed in a tidy navy jacket with silver piping and matching shorts, with a name tag identifying him as James. Every employee of Superstar Cruises wore some variation on that uniform, from the driver who'd picked us up at the Vancouver airport to the woman checking people in over at the gangway.

"That's all I need to know, Ms. Drew," James said. "The Hollywood Suite doesn't have a number."

I watched as he scribbled the letters HS on a bright purple tag, then snapped it onto the handle of my bag. He lifted the suitcase as if it weighed nothing, even though I knew that wasn't the case. I'm no fashion plate, but a girl needs plenty of clothes for a two-week Alaskan cruise! Then he set my bag on a metal cart along with at least a dozen other suitcases, trunks, and duffels.

Meanwhile my friend Bess Marvin was staring up at the ship docked beside us. "Wow," she said. "Big boat."

"Major understatement," I replied. The *Arctic Star* was absolutely massive. We don't see too many cruise ships in our midwestern hometown of River Heights, but I was pretty sure this one was even larger than most.

Just then I heard a scuffle nearby. "Hey, give that back—I don't want to check it!" George Fayne exclaimed as she grabbed a grungy olive-green duffel bag out of another porter's hand.

George is my other best friend. She's also Bess's cousin, though most people find it hard to believe they're related, since the two of them couldn't be more different. Exhibit A? Their luggage. George's consisted of that ugly duffel, a sturdy brown suitcase that looked as if it had been through a demolition derby, and a plain black backpack. Definitely the functional look, just like her short dark hair, faded jeans, and sneakers. Bess, on the other hand, had a matching set of luggage in a nice shade of blue. Tasteful and pulled together, like her sleek, shoulder-length blond hair and linen dress.

The porter took a step back. "Of course, miss," he told George politely. "I only thought—"

"Relax, George," Bess said. "I think you can trust him to get your toothbrush and your days-of-the-week underwear onboard safely."

"My underwear, maybe." George already had the bag unzipped. She scrabbled through the mess inside and finally came up with her laptop and smartphone. "This stuff? I trust no one."

Bess snorted. "Seriously? We're going to be cruising the gorgeous Alaskan waters surrounded by amazing scenery. You're not going to have a lot of time to look for cute kitten videos on YouTube, you know."

"Maybe not," George retorted. "But if we need to research something for Nancy's—"

"Hi, Alan!" I said loudly, cutting her off as I noticed a guy hurrying toward us.

"It's my lucky day!" the guy announced with a big, cheerful grin. "I found my sunglasses. I must've dropped them when we were getting our stuff out of the airport van." He waved the glasses at us, then slid them on and wrapped an arm around Bess's shoulders. "Actually, though, *every* day is my lucky day since I met Beautiful Bess."

George rolled her eyes so hard I was afraid they'd pop right out of her head. "Sooo glad you found your shades, Alan," she said drily. "I was afraid you'd be so busy searching you'd miss the boat."

I hid a smile. About a month earlier, Bess and George and I had been having lunch at one of our favorite cafés when George noticed a guy staring from a nearby table. He was maybe a couple of years older than us, with wavy brown hair and wide-set gray eyes. When he realized he'd been caught, he came over and introduced himself as Alan Thomas, a student at the local university. He apologized for staring and explained that it was because he couldn't take his eyes off Bess.

That kind of thing happens to Bess all the time, so I didn't pay much attention. She's not the type of girl who gets swept off her feet by just anybody.

But apparently Alan wasn't just anybody. He'd taken her on a romantic picnic for their first date, and the two of them had been together ever since. It was nice to see Bess so happy, even if I secretly thought Alan was a little goofy and overly excitable. George thought so too, though with her it wasn't such a secret.

"Need some help with those, buddy?" Alan asked as James returned for Bess's bags. "I can give you a hand. Should I just toss it there on top of Nancy's suitcase?"

"It's quite all right, sir," James replied. "Your entire party is in the Hollywood Suite, right? Just leave your luggage here and we'll take care of it. You might want to head over to the check-in line so you can start enjoying all the fine amenities of the *Arctic Star*."

"Thanks," Bess said. "Come on, you guys. Let's go."

Alan nodded agreeably. "This is so amazing," he said to no one in particular as we headed toward the end of the line. "I never thought a poor college student like me would be taking an Alaskan cruise!"

He wasn't the only one. Just a few short days ago, I'd been wondering what I was going to do with myself for the next month while Ned was off being a camp counselor and my dad was busy with a big case. River Heights is kind of sleepy at the best of times. This summer? It was downright catatonic.

Then Becca Wright had called, sounding frantic. That was my first clue that my summer was about to change. See, Becca is just about the *least* frantic person I've ever known. Just a couple of years out of college, she'd already landed the plum job of assistant cruise director for the maiden voyage of the *Arctic Star*, the flagship vessel of brand-new Superstar Cruises. Having known Becca for years, I was sure that was mostly due to her work ethic and friendly, upbeat personality. Although I'm sure it didn't hurt that her grandfather had been a bigwig executive at the venerable Jubilee Cruise Lines. He'd retired a few years back, but he still knew just about everyone in the business.

So why the frantic call? Some suspicious things were happening at Superstar Cruises, and Becca was afraid someone might be up to no good. Naturally, that made her think of me. See, my thing is solving mysteries. Big ones. And small ones, like the case where I'd first met Becca, which had involved finding her family's runaway dog. And everything in between.

So which kind of case was this? I wondered, glancing up again at the gleaming white ship looming over the dock. Was someone really out to mess with Superstar Cruises like Becca seemed to think? Or was it just new-job jitters and a little bad luck?

"Earth to Nancy!" Alan waved a hand in front of

my face, grinning. "You look a little nervous. Not worried about getting seasick, are you?"

"Nope." I smiled back at him. Real mystery or not, I was glad that Becca had called. My friends and I were about to set out on the all-expenses-paid cruise of a lifetime!

The four of us joined the line waiting to board, which was growing with every passing second. George stood on tiptoes, hopping from one foot to the other as she tried to see how many people were in front of us.

"Hey, shouldn't there be a special VIP line or something?" she complained. "I mean, we're in the Hollywood Suite! We shouldn't have to wait in line with everyone else."

"Yeah." Alan chuckled. "Plus, we're contest winners! That should count for something, right?"

"Um, the line's moving pretty fast. I'm sure we'll be aboard soon," I said quickly. The last thing we needed was for Alan to start blabbing to the ship's employees about the whole contest-winner thing. Mainly because it wasn't true.

Bess shifted her handbag to her other shoulder and pulled out a packet of paperwork. "Does everyone have their tickets and passports handy? Nancy?"

"Why are you looking at me?" I said. "I'm not *that* forgetful, even when I'm—" I caught myself just in time, swallowing the last few words: *even when I'm investigating a case.* "Um, even when I've just crossed a couple of time zones," I finished lamely, shooting a look at Alan.

Luckily, he wasn't paying attention. He was digging into the pockets of his Bermuda shorts.

"Uh-oh," he said. "I think I left my passport in one of my bags. I'd better go grab it before they load it onto the ship."

He rushed off, disappearing into the throng of passengers, porters, and bystanders on the dock. George watched him go with a sigh.

"Okay, this is already getting old," she said. "Shouldn't we just let him in on the secret already? Alan's a huge goody-two-shoes nerd—I'm sure we can trust him not to tell anyone we're really here to solve a mystery."

"Shh," I cautioned her, glancing around quickly.

"Don't call him a nerd," Bess added with a glare. "He's just . . . enthusiastic about things."

"Yeah. Like I said. Nerd," George said.

I ignored their bickering, realizing I didn't have to worry about anyone overhearing us at the moment. A red-haired young man had just arrived at the dock, and about a dozen other people, from little kids to an old woman with a walker, were pushing and shoving and laughing loudly as they all tried to fling themselves at him at once. Almost every single one of them had bright red hair and freckles.

Bess followed my gaze. "Family reunion?" she murmured.

"Brilliant deduction, detective." I grinned at her, then turned to George. "We can't tell anyone why we're really here," I reminded her quietly. "Not even Alan. We promised Becca, remember? Besides, we've really only known Alan for a few weeks."

"Oh, please." Bess shook her head. "What do you think he's going to do? Call the *New York Times* so they can publish all your clues?"

"No, of course not." I glanced over my shoulder to make sure Alan wasn't returning yet. "But he's not exactly Mr. Introvert. We don't need him blurting out something at the wrong time, even by accident."

"Whatever." George didn't look entirely convinced. "Guess we'd better talk about the case while we can, then. What's your plan?"

"The first thing I need to do is talk to Becca," I said. "All she told me on the phone was that there'd been a few troubling incidents in the couple of weeks leading up to this cruise, including some threatening e-mails or something. Oh, and the Brock thing, of course."

Bess sighed dreamily. "I can't believe we almost got to be on the same cruise ship as Brock Walker!"

"No, we didn't," I said. "That's why Becca called us in to help, remember? According to her, Brock Walker was supposed to put the 'superstar' in Superstar Cruises. I guess that's their gimmick—passengers being able to rub elbows with superstars. So when he canceled less than five days before departure, she knew it was bad news. Then when she heard it was because someone was sending threatening e-mails to his family . . ."

"Sounds like a mystery to me," George agreed, kicking at a loose board on the dock.

I nodded slowly, still not entirely convinced. Brock Walker was an A-list actor who'd starred in a popular series of bad-boy comedy-action films. But in real life he was supposed to be a hard-working, down-to-earth family man, married to his high school sweetheart, with a couple of kids. Definitely *not* the type to flake out on a commitment, at least according to his reputation.

"I wonder what they told the paying passengers." Bess glanced around. "Especially since the rest of the entertainment is C-list at best."

George patted her laptop, which she'd slung over her shoulder in its case. "I checked earlier today— Brock put out a statement saying it was a scheduling conflict."

"Yeah." I shuffled forward as the line continued to move. "But Becca said he's really mad about the threats. He told the CEO of Superstar Cruises that if the company doesn't figure out who did it, he'll tell everyone the truth."

"Bummer." George shrugged. "But that sounds like a job for the cops or the FBI or someone like that."

"I know." I sighed. "The trouble is, the CEO is afraid that any bad publicity involving police investigations might scare off passengers and sink the company." I chuckled, realizing what I'd just said. "So to speak. Anyway, that's why we're here—undercover. The CEO used to work with Becca's grandfather, so I guess she and Becca are practically like family. Since it was too late to re-book Brock's suite, Becca talked her into flying us out and letting us stay there while we keep an eye on things."

"Which is totally awesome," George said with a grin, shooting a look up at the ship. "I'm not sure about this whole cruise thing, but I've always wanted to see Alaska!"

"So what else did Becca tell you?" Bess asked me. "You said there were some other suspicious incidents."

I nodded. "That's what she said, but she didn't go into much detail. Just mentioned something about threatening e-mails, and some prelaunch mishaps. She's supposed to fill me in when I see her. Once we know more, maybe we'll be able to—"

I stopped short as Bess cleared her throat loudly. A moment later Alan arrived, apologizing to the people in line behind us.

"Found it," he announced, holding up his passport. "I got there just in time—that porter was about to roll our cart away."

I forced a smile. Having Alan along was definitely going to make things more difficult. That hadn't been part of the original plan.

But when he'd heard that the three of us had won a free cruise to Alaska in a four-bedroom suite—cover story, remember?—he'd begged to come along. As an environmental studies student at the university in River Heights, he'd pointed out that Alaska was the perfect place to get a jump-start on his sophomore-year research project, and he'd never be able to afford that kind of trip on a college kid's budget. Especially when he lavished what little spare cash he had on his new girlfriend, Bess.

Okay, so he hadn't *actually* mentioned that last part. He hadn't had to. Bess had invited him along and told us we'd just have to deal with it. The girl seems sweet and agreeable most of the time, but she's got a backbone of steel when the situation calls for it.

Soon we were inside, being checked in and issued our ship ID cards. "Enjoy your time with Superstar Cruises!" the smiling employee told us.

As we thanked her and stepped away, I nudged Bess in the side. "Can you distract you-know-who for a while?" I whispered. "I want to look for Becca."

"Leave it to me," Bess murmured back.

Alan had just moved away from the check-in desk to tuck his ID into his wallet, but he looked up quickly. "Did you say something?" he asked Bess.

She stepped over and looped her arm through his. "I was just telling Nancy we'd meet her and George at the suite later," she told him with a flirty little tilt of her head. "Want to go for a walk to check out the ship?"

She didn't have to ask twice. Seconds later they were strolling out of the check-in area hand in hand. George shook her head as she watched them go.

"That guy's got it bad," she said. "I really don't know what Bess sees in him, though."

"That's a mystery for another day." I headed out after them. "Let's not waste time. Becca said we'd probably find her on the main deck."

George glanced around as we emerged into what appeared to be a sort of lobby area. It was carpeted in red, with murals on the walls depicting famous Hollywood landmarks. A pair of winding, carpeted staircases with gleaming mahogany banisters led upward, with a sign in between that showed the layout of the entire ship.

I barely had time to glance at the sign before a smiling young female employee rushed toward us. She was dressed in shorts and a piped vest and was holding a tray of tall, frosty glasses with colorful straws and umbrellas sticking out of them.

"Welcome to the *Arctic Star*," she gushed. "Would

you ladies care for a complimentary Superstar smoothie? They're made with a refreshing fruit mixture, including real Alaskan wild blueberries. A specialty of the ship!"

George was already reaching for a glass. She's not the type to turn down anything free. "Thanks," she said, then took a sip. "Hey, Nancy, you've got to try this! It's awesome!"

"Thanks, but I'm not thirsty," I told the waitress. Grabbing George's arm, I dragged her toward the stairs. "Focus, okay?"

"Whatever. A girl's got to stay hydrated." George took another big sip of her smoothie as we hurried upstairs.

A couple of flights up, we found the lido deck. It was a partially shaded area spanning the entire width of the ship, and appeared to be where all the action was at the moment. As we emerged out of the stairwell, we almost crashed into another employee. This one was a lean, tanned man in his late twenties with slicked-back brown hair.

"Welcome aboard, ladies," he said with a toothy grin.

"My name's Scott, and I'm one of your shore excursion specialists. Our first stop the day after tomorrow will be Ketchikan, where you'll have the chance to experience anything from a flight-seeing trip to the fjords to the Great Alaskan Lumberjack Show or . . ."

There was more, but I didn't hear it. I'd just spotted Becca halfway across the deck chatting with some passengers, looking trim and professional in her silver-piped navy jacket and skirt.

"Sounds great," I blurted out, interrupting Shore Excursion Scott's description of kayaking in Tongass National Forest. "We'll get back to you on that, okay?"

"Save me a spot on those kayaks," George called over her shoulder as I yanked her away.

"Ladies!" someone called out cheerfully. Suddenly we found our path blocked by yet another uniformed employee. This one was a short, skinny guy with a wild tuft of blond hair and a slightly manic twinkle in his big blue eyes. "Hollywood Suite, right?" he asked.

"Yeah." George sounded surprised. "How'd you know that?"

"Oh, they send us photos of our guests ahead of time. You're Nancy and you're Georgia, right?"

"George," George corrected with a grimace. She hates her real name. "Call me George."

"George it is!" The guy seemed as if he couldn't stand still. He sort of bounded back and forth in front of us. It reminded me of my neighbor's over-enthusiastic golden retriever. "My name's Max. Oh, but you probably figured that out already, right?" He grinned and pointed to his name tag. "I'll be your personal butler."

"Our what?" I said.

"Whoa!" George exclaimed. "Seriously? We get a *butler*?"

"Absolutely." Max nodded vigorously. "Each of our luxury suites has its own dedicated staff, including a butler and two maids, to make sure your trip is as pleasant and comfortable as possible. You can call on me day or night for all your needs."

"Cool," I said briskly. Max seemed like a really nice guy, but I was feeling impatient. Over his shoulder, I could see Becca moving on to another set of passengers. "We'll get back to you, okay?"

But Max had already whipped out a handful of pamphlets. "Here's a partial list of our available services to get you started," he said brightly. "Our room service menu, the shipboard activity schedule, spa services, our exclusive pillow menu . . ."

George was already examining the pamphlets eagerly. I could see that it wasn't going to be easy to shake Max.

Then I had an idea. I grabbed one of the pamphlets. "Er, the pillow menu, huh?" I said. "Come to think of it, I can't sleep well on anything but a . . . um . . ." I quickly scanned the list. "A buckwheat pillow. Do you think you could find me one right now? I might need to take a nap soon."

"Certainly, Ms. Drew!" Max beamed as if I'd just asked him to be my best friend. "I'll take care of it right away. Just text me if you need anything else." He handed us each a card with his name and number on it, then scurried away.

"Wow," George said. "A real butler! This is awesome. Maybe I should tell him to get me a special fancy pillow while he's at it."

"Forget it," I said, slapping her hand as she reached for her cell phone. "Becca. Now."

This time we actually made it over to her. I hadn't seen her in a couple of years, but she looked pretty much the same—curly dark hair, sparkling brown eyes, a quick smile. She was chatting with a rather weary-looking couple in their thirties. The man wore a T-shirt with the Canadian flag on it, and the woman was keeping one eye on the eight-year-old boy dribbling a soccer ball nearby.

"Careful, Tobias," she called, interrupting something Becca was saying about the dinner schedule. "We don't want to be a bother to the other passengers."

"Maybe *you* don't," the boy retorted, sticking out his tongue. "I told you I didn't want to come on this stupid ship!" With that, he kicked the ball into a column. It bounced off and almost hit a passing woman.

"Wow," George murmured in my ear. "Brat much?"

Becca's smile never wavered. She glanced toward me and George briefly, then returned her focus to the parents. "We have lots of activities for our youngest guests," she told them. "Perhaps your son would enjoy checking out the rock-climbing wall or the arcade. There's also a kids' tour of the ship scheduled for first thing tomorrow morning. One of our youth activities coordinators can give you all the details if you're interested."

She gestured toward a good-looking young Asian guy standing nearby. Tobias's parents thanked her, then grabbed their son's hand and dragged him toward the youth coordinator.

"Nancy!" Becca exclaimed as soon as they were out of earshot. "Thank goodness you made it. Hi, George." She glanced around. "Where's Bess?"

"She's, uh, busy right now." I didn't want to waste time explaining about Alan. I knew we probably only had a few seconds before Becca had to return to duty. "So when do you want to meet to talk?"

"Soon." Becca shot a cautious look around, her smile fading. Then she lowered her voice. "Something else has happened, but I don't have time to fill you in now. Can you meet me at my office later?"

"Sure. Where is it?"

She was writing the deck and cabin numbers down on her card when a sudden, shrill scream rang out from somewhere farther along the huge deck area.

"What was that?" George exclaimed.

Becca instantly looked worried. "I don't know, but I hope—"

Before she could finish, someone let out a shout. "Help! There's a bloody body in the pool!"

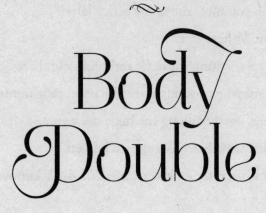

CHAPTER TWO

Body Double

"WHAT?" BECCA BLURTED OUT, HER FACE going pale. Without another word, she rushed off in the direction of the commotion.

I traded a worried glance with George. "Come on," I said. "Let's go see what's happening."

We followed the crowd and soon emerged onto a sunny, open-air part of the deck dominated by a large free-form pool. It was a riot of fountains, slides, and potted palms.

But nobody was looking at any of that. Everyone's focus was on the blond woman's pale, still form floating facedown in a widening reddish circle!

My heart pounded, and for a second I felt dizzy. I've been involved in a lot of mysteries. But very few of them involved bloody bodies of any kind. Somehow I'd just about convinced myself that Becca was imagining trouble where it didn't exist, that this was really just going to be a fun, free vacation with a little sleuthing on the side. But now? Maybe not so much.

"Oh, gross," George exclaimed, watching as a lifeguard-looking guy in silver-piped trunks dove into the pool and sliced through the pinkish-tinged water. "There's a ton of blood!"

Before I could answer, the lifeguard reached the body. He grabbed one arm, then jumped back. "Hey, it's not a real person!" he called out, sounding confused. "It's just a mannequin!"

Realizing I'd been holding my breath, I blew it out in a big *whoosh*. "Thank goodness." I glanced around for Becca and spotted her nearby. Hurrying over, I touched her on the arm. "Do you have any idea what this is all about?"

She shook her head, looking grim. Meanwhile George was staring at a young couple nearby. A pretty, willowy blonde in her midtwenties was huddled in the arms of a tall, handsome, broad-shouldered man around the same age.

"Whoa," George commented. "Looks like that girl is pretty freaked out."

Most of the people near the pool looked more excited or curious than scared now as they chattered and laughed about what had happened. But the young woman was shaking and moaning, looking really upset.

"I just met those two a few minutes ago," Becca said. "They're honeymooners. Vince and Lacey, from Iowa."

Pasting a smile on her face, she hurried over, George and me on her heels. The woman—Lacey—looked up as Becca approached. Her big hazel eyes were brimming with tears.

"Oh, this is terrible!" she moaned. "What kind of cruise *is* this?"

"It's okay, sweetheart," her husband said, stroking her hair gently. "It'll be okay."

"No!" Lacey cried, sounding borderline hysterical. "It's a bad sign, I know it!" She glanced up at Vince. "I knew we should have gone with Jubilee Cruises after all!"

Becca bit her lip. "Please don't be upset," she said. "This is just a, um, misunderstanding. Of some sort. I think."

I cringed. Becca was one of the most tactful and gracious people I'd ever met. But she had her work cut out for her. Sure, maybe Lacey was overreacting a little. But who expects to see a body—even a fake one—on their honeymoon cruise? Or *any* cruise, for that matter?

Becca was still trying to soothe the hysterical honeymooner when a handsome man in his forties arrived. He was wearing a crisp navy-and-silver uniform and a name tag that read MARCELO: CRUISE DIRECTOR.

"I guess that's Becca's boss," I whispered to George.

Within moments Marcelo had assessed the situation and hustled the couple off for a complimentary beverage. Becca and the other employees started shooing the rest of the hangers-on out of the pool area.

"Should we take a look around while everyone's distracted?" George whispered.

"You read my mind."

We hurried closer to the pool. The lifeguard had just dragged the mannequin to the edge.

"So where'd that thing come from?" I asked him, keeping my tone casual.

He hoisted the mannequin out of the water by the straps of its floral bikini, brushing off his hands as it landed on the concrete edge with a clatter. Then he glanced up at me.

"It's nothing to worry about, miss," he said politely. "Looks like it came from one of the onboard shops."

As he dove back in to retrieve the floating wig, I leaned closer to the mannequin. There didn't seem to be anything unusual about it that I could see. It was just a plastic figure with a blank white face, like the ones occupying the picture windows of countless stores all over the world.

George was staring out at the water. "So that's

obviously not real blood, either," she said. "What do you think it is?"

"It looks kind of pink, actually." I stepped to the edge of the pool and leaned down for a closer look "Hmm. Smells like raspberry?"

George stepped back and glanced around. Spotting a shiny silver trash receptacle nearby, she hurried over and peered inside.

"Aha!" she said, reaching in and pulling something out. "You were close. It's cherry, actually."

I looked at what she'd found. It was a large plastic tub of powdered drink mix. Cherry flavor. Empty.

"Fake blood to go with a fake body," I mused. "Why would someone do that? And then leave the evidence nearby?"

"Who knows?" George said. "Maybe . . ."

She let her voice trail off. Someone was hurrying toward us. It was a short, pointy-chinned woman in her twenties. She was wearing a man's fedora and a thrift-store floral granny dress, along with bright purple plastic earrings and thick, square-framed black glasses. A snazzy-looking laptop was tucked under one thin, pasty-pale arm.

"Isn't this crazy?" she exclaimed, shoving her glasses up her nose and grinning at us as if we were her best friends. "It's like one of those murder-mystery cruises or something, except nobody knew it was going to happen! Bonus, right?"

"Um, yeah, okay," George said.

"By the way, I'm Wendy. Wendy Webster." She stuck out her hand. "I'm a travel blogger. Wendy's Wanderings—maybe you've heard of it? It's like the coolest new travel blog, according to the coolest bloggers."

"I'm Nancy, and this is George." I shook her hand. "Sorry, I don't really follow blogs too much."

That seemed to take her by surprise. She stared at me over the tops of her glasses for a second, studying me as if I were an alien species.

Finally she shrugged. "Oh. You're retro, huh? That's cool," she said. "Anyway, I thought this was going to be just another boring cruise, you know? Did you guys, like, see what happened?"

"Nope," George said. "We're clueless."

I shot her a look, and she smiled back innocently. I was already trying to come up with an excuse to get away from Blogger Wendy. We weren't going to be able to do much investigating with her hanging around.

Just then a pair of young men in Superstar uniforms hurried over. "Excuse us, ladies," one of them said. "Could we ask you to please vacate the pool area? We just need time to clean up, and will reopen the pool as soon as we can."

The second young man nodded. "They're serving complimentary smoothies in the atrium lounge," he added, gesturing.

Wendy's eyes lit up. "Free smoothies?" she said. "I'm so there! Come on, girls!"

I grabbed George's arm to stop her from following. "Let her go," I hissed. "You already had your free smoothie, remember?"

We drifted toward the lounge slowly, staying behind the rest of the crowd so we could talk. "So that was weird," George said.

"What? Wendy?"

She laughed. "Yeah, her too. But I meant the pool thing. Think they'll call the cops?"

"I don't know." I shrugged. "If they do, it could delay our departure. Based on what Becca told me, I don't think the CEO would like that. Bad publicity, remember?"

"Yeah. Plus, nobody actually got hurt or anything." George grimaced. "Uh-oh—incoming."

Following her gaze, I saw Alan striding toward us, with Bess at his heels. "There you are!" Alan exclaimed. "Did you hear about the fake dead body in the pool?"

"Yeah." I traded a look with Bess, who raised one eyebrow curiously. "We heard."

Luckily, Alan didn't seem interested in discussing it. "Anyway, we've been looking all over for you two," he said. "Bess wants to check out our suite, but I thought we should wait until we're all together. Should we go find it now?"

"Sure, let's go," I replied. "Anyone know how to get there?"

"I think it's this way." Alan hurried off toward the nearest set of elevators.

As it turned out, he had no idea how to find our suite. We wandered around for a while, heading down a couple of levels via elevator and then following signs pointing us down one long, windowless hallway after another. There weren't many people down there—I guessed most of the passengers were upstairs watching the ship prepare to pull out of Vancouver's busy harbor.

"Wow." George was panting slightly as we jogged up a staircase. "This ship seems even bigger on the inside than it does on the outside."

"We could be lost for days before anyone could find us." Alan wriggled his fingers in a spooky way.

I paused at the intersection of two hallways. The one we'd been following was lined with numbered cabin doors. The other was narrower and shorter, with a sign on the wall reading GALLEY—EMPLOYEES ONLY.

"Maybe we should go ask someone back there," I said, gesturing toward the sign.

"Aw, you're giving up so soon?" Alan grinned. "Where's your sense of adventure, Nancy?"

"I'm not sure. I think I lost it a few levels back," I joked weakly.

We hurried down the hallway. As we neared the corner, I heard voices ahead.

"Good, sounds like there's someone back there," Bess said.

The voices stopped abruptly as we came into sight. Three men turned to stare at us in surprise. Two of them wore Superstar Cruises uniforms. One was holding a broom and dustpan, while the other had a white kitchen apron tied on over his navy shorts. The third man appeared to be a passenger. He was in his fifties and heavyset, with a droopy mustache and prominent jowls. He was dressed in Bermuda shorts and a Hawaiian shirt.

"Excuse me," I said. "We're looking for our suite, and we're kind of lost."

"Me too," Mr. Hawaiian Shirt said, the corners of his mouth turning up beneath his mustache. "This ship is a giant maze, isn't it? It's like a floating fiefdom!" He chortled and slapped one of the employees on the back. "These fellows were just helping me find my way. Isn't that right?"

"Yes, sir," the guy with the apron said. He looked at the other employee, who smiled uncertainly and scurried off in the opposite direction. "What's your cabin number?"

Was it my imagination, or did the kitchen worker look sort of anxious? It was hard to tell in the dimly lit hallway.

"We're in the Hollywood Suite," George told him.

"*Ooh la la!*" Mr. Hawaiian Shirt whistled. "Sounds fancy! See you youngsters around." He nodded at us, then strolled off and disappeared around the corner.

The remaining employee gave us directions. "Enjoy your time with Superstar Cruises," he finished softly. Then he turned and hurried off.

"That was a little strange, wasn't it?" Bess said when he was gone.

"Strange? How do you mean?" Alan put an arm around her.

"Nothing," George said quickly. "Um, I mean, I didn't notice anything."

Alan shrugged. "Okay. Now come on, let's see if we can find our rooms this time!"

When we finally found it, the Hollywood Suite turned out to be pretty spectacular. We entered through a marble-floored foyer into a two-story living room with a grand piano, floor-to-ceiling windows, and a sliding door leading onto a roomy private balcony. George hurried toward the balcony, which offered a great view of Vancouver shrinking behind us as the ship chugged away. When she reached the glass doors leading out there, she gasped.

"Whoa!" she exclaimed. "We have our own hot tub!"

Just then one of the other doors opened, and Max the butler hurried out. "You found it!" he exclaimed with a bright smile. "I was just starting to worry. Nancy, your buckwheat pillow should be here any minute."

"Buckwheat pillow?" Bess echoed, shooting me a look.

I ignored her. "Thanks, Max," I said. "I really appreciate it."

"That's what I'm here for!" He hurried over to the pile of luggage stacked near the piano. "Now if you tell me who's going to be in which room, I can assist you with your unpacking if you like."

"Thanks," I said again. "But I'm sure we can . . ."

My voice trailed off. I'd just noticed something.

"Hey," I said. "Where's my suitcase?"

CHAPTER THREE

Rumors and Surprises

I SHOVED GEORGE'S DUFFEL ASIDE FOR A better look at the rest of the luggage. My friends' stuff was all there, along with the big hobo bag I'd used as a carry-on for the plane. But there was no sign of my green suitcase.

"Oh, dear," Max said. "Is something missing?"

"Only the bag with most of my stuff in it," I exclaimed.

"Are you sure it's not here somewhere?" Bess

glanced around the main room. "We watched the porter label it ourselves, remember?"

"Of course I remember." My words came out clipped and short, and I took a deep breath and tried to compose myself before continuing. "Who should I call about this?" I asked Max.

"Me," he declared, patting me on the arm. "Don't fret, Ms. Drew, I'll take care of it right away. There must have been some kind of mix-up with the room tags."

That didn't seem possible, since Bess was right— I'd seen the porter label the bag myself. But I didn't get a chance to say so, since Max was already rushing out of the suite with his cell phone pressed to his ear, leaving the door standing open behind him.

"It's okay, Nancy," Alan said. "I'm sure your bag's around somewhere."

"Yeah," George said. "It's not like we're at the airport and it accidentally got on a plane headed to Timbuktu. The worst that could happen is they dropped it in the harbor." She smirked.

"Very funny," I growled.

George and Bess traded a surprised look. "Chill, Nance," George said. "It's not that big a deal. Max will track it down."

I took another deep breath, realizing she was right. What was going on with me, anyway? I wasn't normally the type to freak out over minor mishaps like this.

Maybe seeing that body shook me more than I realized, I thought. *Even if it wasn't real . . .*

That made my mind jump from my suitcase to a different kind of case. I wished I could talk to my friends about what had happened by the pool. But we couldn't talk freely with Alan around. He'd just sat down at the piano and was picking out "Jingle Bells" with one finger.

"What should we do now?" Bess asked. "Do you guys want to start unpacking, or—"

She was cut off by a sudden loud, terrified shriek from just outside the suite.

"Who was that?" Alan exclaimed.

I was already rushing toward the door. When I

burst into the hallway, a young woman was standing in front of the next door down, looking horrified. She was wearing a Superstar uniform and clutching a stack of folded towels to her chest.

"Is everyone okay?" Bess yelped, running out of the suite behind me.

My gaze had already shot from the maid to the kid crouched on the floor just across the hall. He had his back to us at first, but when he glanced back over his shoulder, my eyes widened.

"You!" I blurted out.

It was the bratty eight-year-old I'd seen earlier. What was his name again?

"Hey, it's Tobias!" George exclaimed as she skidded out into the hallway and stopped short.

"That's my name, don't wear it out," the kid snapped.

By now the maid had lowered the towels, revealing a name tag that identified her as Iris. "Oh!" she gasped. "I'm so sorry. He—he just startled me."

Tobias glared at her. "You practically broke my eardrum, screaming like that," he said. "I should sue you.

Then I could use the money to hire a helicopter to fly me out of here."

Just then a nearby door swung open. Tobias's father emerged. "What's going on out here?" he asked.

"Nothing." Tobias stood up, quickly shoving one hand deep into the pocket of his baggy cargo shorts.

"Hmm." His father leaned forward to peer at the maid's name tag. "Iris, is it? Is Tobias causing trouble?"

"No, no, no, not at all, sir." Iris took a quick step backward, clutching the towels to her again. "It's completely my fault, really. I wasn't paying enough attention to where I was going."

Tobias's father didn't look convinced as he looked over at his son. "Well, I hope he's behaving better than he was earlier today. It seems he's feeling a little, uh, cranky right now because he didn't want to come on this cruise."

"Yeah." Tobias scowled. "I wanted to go to Galaxy X. *That's* what I call a cool vacation. Not some stupid boat."

"That's enough, son." His father grabbed Tobias by the arm and pulled him into the room. "Sorry," he added once more before shutting the door.

"Wow," Bess said. "That kid's pretty obnoxious."

"Yeah, we sort of met him earlier." I glanced at the maid. "Are you okay? What'd he do to scare you?"

"Nothing." Iris shrugged. "Like I said, he just startled me. Excuse me, I'd better get back to work."

She turned and hurried off down the hall. "Excitement's over," Alan announced. "Better get back to my music." He headed back into the suite.

But I was still staring off after the maid. "She was acting kind of oddly, wasn't she?"

Bess grinned. "First your misplaced bag, and now this?" she teased. "You don't have to look for mysteries *everywhere*, Nancy."

"Yeah." George looked at the door to make sure Alan was out of earshot. "It's not like some eight-year-old is sending threatening e-mails to Brock Walker and planting fake bodies in pools."

I smiled. "I guess you're right."

We went back inside. Alan was at the piano again. Bess made a beeline for the luggage.

"I guess we might as well start unpacking," she said, picking up her cosmetics case.

I glanced at my pathetic little carry-on. There didn't seem to be much point in trying to settle in until Max found my suitcase. Besides, I had more important things to do.

"You guys go ahead," I said. "I think I'll go pick up a toothbrush in one of the onboard shops. Just in case."

"But I'm sure Max will—" George began.

"I know," I cut her off. "But I feel like taking a walk. I'll be back soon."

As soon as I was away from the suite, I pulled out my phone and texted Becca to see if she was free to talk. She texted back immediately, telling me she was in her office.

The office turned out to be a small, poorly lit, windowless cabin on one of the lower levels. It was crammed with two large desks and several filing cabinets. Becca was hunched over a laptop at one of the desks, typing frantically. When I knocked softly on the door frame, she glanced up and pushed her hair out of her eyes.

"Nancy!" she exclaimed. "Come on in. I'm just typing up the daily newsletter." She hit a button on the keyboard and grimaced. "I'm a little behind, thanks to all the commotion earlier."

"Yeah, about that." I shut the door behind me and perched on the edge of the other desk. "Did you find out anything else about what happened?"

Becca sighed. "Marcelo and the captain contacted HQ to see what to do. Verity told them to treat it as a prank and just move on."

"Verity?" I echoed.

"Verity Salinas," Becca said. "She's the CEO of Superstar Cruises."

"Oh, right. I don't think you mentioned her name before." I nodded. "So she doesn't want to involve the local police?"

Becca shook her head. "She said to let ship security handle it. They already did a little investigating and figured out that the mannequin came from one of the clothing shops on the promenade level. And that pink stuff in the water was drink mix swiped from the snack bar in the kids' playground area."

"Did they figure out who did it?"

"Not yet." Becca raked a hand through her hair, making her curls stand up wildly. "But I suppose there's no real harm done. We offered the newlyweds a free shore excursion in Ketchikan, and I think that satisfied them."

"Vince and Lacey," I said, remembering the frightened young woman and her new husband.

"Right." Becca smiled at me. "Good memory for names, Nancy. Maybe you should work in the cruise industry."

"I don't think so," I joked in return. "Bess and George could tell you I only remember details when they have to do with a case. Otherwise, I can't even find my keys most of the time!"

Becca chuckled, then glanced at her computer screen. "I don't have much time," she said. "But I guess I should fill you in on the latest trouble." She picked at a chipped spot on the corner of the desk. "I just found out today about a rumor circulating among the house-keeping staff."

"What kind of rumor?"

"That the company is already bankrupt, so nobody's going to get paid." Becca shook her head. "It's not true, obviously. The housekeeping supervisors managed to calm everybody down for now, but nobody seems to know where the rumor started. It's just one more thing going wrong. . . ."

"Yeah, that's what I wanted to talk to you about," I said. "You told me about the threat to Brock's family that made him cancel, and that some other bad stuff had happened. What's the other stuff?"

"Well, it started with an e-mail I got a couple of weeks ago."

"What did it say?"

Becca shrugged. "Just something about how I should back out of this cruise if I knew what was good for me, or something like that. But that's not all. There were a few incidents in the last couple of weeks. A shipment of supplies got lost in the mail and never turned up. Three of the ship's cooks quit a week before departure. Stuff like that."

"Okay, the e-mail sounds weird," I said. "But the other problems could just be ordinary bad luck or whatever, couldn't they?"

"Maybe. But what about the body in the pool? It takes more than bad luck to make something like that happen."

"Good point." I drummed my fingers on the desk, thinking over what she'd told me. "We should try to figure out possible motives. The e-mail makes it seem like someone's trying to scare you—maybe someone who's envious of your cool new job. Do you have any enemies onboard or any you can think of?"

"Not that I know of." Becca looked alarmed. "Do you really think someone's targeting me personally?"

"Not necessarily," I assured her. "I mean, for all we know other people could've received threatening e-mails too. Maybe someone's after your boss—Marcelo, is it?"

Becca looked dubious. "Everyone loves Marcelo. He's been in the business for years and has never had an enemy that I've heard of."

"Then maybe it's the captain," I said. "Or Verity, or

the company as a whole. Or maybe someone we haven't even thought of yet."

Becca smiled wryly. "That really narrows it down."

"Sorry." I chuckled. "I've learned it's better not to rule anything out without solid evidence. We need to keep thinking about motives and—"

I cut myself off as the door flew open. A woman stood in the doorway. She was in her early thirties, tall, blond, and attractive, dressed in a navy-blue evening gown with silver jewelry.

"There you are, Becca," the woman said in a husky, rather brusque voice tinged with an Eastern European accent. "Marcelo's wondering where you are—it's nearly dinnertime, you know."

"Oops!" Becca glanced at her watch and jumped to her feet. "Sorry, Tatjana. I lost track of time." She shot me an apologetic look. "I need to change into my evening clothes so I can greet guests at dinner. We'll have to chat later."

Tatjana glanced at me, her gray eyes curious. "Can I help with something?"

"No, I'm fine." I smiled at her. She shrugged and turned to follow Becca out of the office.

When I got back to the Hollywood Suite, I was relieved to see my suitcase standing near the piano. "You found it!" I exclaimed.

Max hurried over from the kitchenette in the corner, dusting a drinking glass and grinning at me. "Of course I did! I'm here to take care of you." He gestured to the yellow numbered tag hanging from the handle. "It got mislabeled somehow and ended up in an interior cabin at the opposite end of the ship. I'm so sorry for the inconvenience."

"It's okay," I said automatically. But I was frowning at that tag, feeling puzzled and a little uneasy. I'd watched the porter clip on the proper purple tag myself. How had it ended up being switched with this yellow one?

But I shook off the thought as quickly as it came. These things happened. It would be easy enough for one of those plastic tags to pop off while the busy porters were moving bags around.

Just then Bess hurried into the main room. She looked lovely in a dove-gray dress and heels.

"You're back!" she said. "Hurry up and get changed. And don't forget to wear something nice—Max says people usually dress up for the first night's dinner."

"Okay. Did you break the news to George?"

Bess grimaced. "I've been working on her for the past half hour. I think I finally convinced her that shorts and flip-flops are *not* proper dinner attire. But I'd better go make sure she didn't 'accidentally' spill something on the dress I loaned her."

I laughed. "I'll be ready in a few minutes," I promised.

My bedroom was beautifully designed, with a built-in bed, a large dresser, and a chair. I tossed my suitcase on the bed and clicked the latches. As my fingers brushed that yellow tag I hesitated briefly, once again wondering how the mix-up had happened. Then I shook my head and opened the suitcase.

My neatly folded clothes were still inside, held in place by a couple of nylon straps. Tucked into one of the straps was a ragged scrap of paper folded in two.

What's that? I thought. I hadn't put anything like that in there. I was positive.

I picked it up and unfolded it. When I saw the message written in handwritten block letters, I gasped.

I HOPE U GET LOST JUST LIKE UR BAG—& THAT U STAY LOST!

CHAPTER FOUR

Dinner Is Served

"I FEEL LIKE A GIANT GRAPE," GEORGE complained, tugging at the hem of her plum-colored wraparound dress. Well, technically speaking, it was *Bess's* dress. But George was wearing it. And she wasn't happy about it.

"I can't believe you didn't pack a single dressy outfit," Bess retorted. "Didn't you ever see a rerun of *The Love Boat*? Remember *Titanic*? People dress up on cruises. It's, like, a *thing*."

"Now, now, ladies," Alan put in soothingly. "You look fabulous—all three of you."

I forced a brief smile as Bess thanked him and George rolled her eyes. But I wasn't paying much attention to the conversation as we walked through the narrow halls leading from our suite to the dining room. I was still focused on that threatening note. Who could have left it in my suitcase? And why?

"It doesn't make sense," I murmured.

"What was that, Nancy?" Alan asked.

"Um, nothing," I said. "I mean, I said I hope the food's good. I'm hungry."

The others started chatting about the food, and my mind drifted again. Why would someone leave me a note like that? Before today, I'd never met a soul on board this cruise ship other than Bess, George, Alan, and Becca. Why would anyone have any reason to threaten me?

As careful as I'd been, I supposed it was possible that someone had found out why I was really there. Maybe that blogger Wendy overheard George and me talking about the case. Becca's coworker, Tatjana, could have lurked outside Becca's office long enough to eavesdrop. Someone could have hacked into Becca's e-mail account and read her messages to me last week. Far-fetched, but you never knew . . .

I shivered. Had my cover been blown? Was I trapped on a ship with someone who was out to get me?

"Wow," George said, stopping short so that I almost crashed into her. "This place is huge!"

I peered around her. We were in the entrance to the ship's main dining room, a cavernous space on one of the upper decks. It was plush and opulent, with crystal chandeliers glittering overhead and red-and-gold upholstery everywhere else. The smells of various types of food drifted toward us, along with the buzz of many conversations, the tinkle of glassware, and an occasional burst of laughter.

When we stepped inside, Alan craned his neck upward. "Check it out," he said with a grin. "Dinner beneath the stars—literally!"

Following his gaze, I saw that there were several skylights between the chandeliers. Through the closest one, we could see a large swath of the evening sky—

twilight blue washed with pink. Countless stars were just twinkling into sight, looking much closer than they did back home in River Heights.

"Gorgeous," I said, the view distracting me from my worries. At least for a moment.

A smiling hostess hurried toward us. "You're at table seventeen," she said after checking our ship IDs. "Follow me, please."

Table seventeen turned out to be a large round table set for nine located near the center of the room. When we arrived, three women in their sixties or seventies were already seated there.

"Welcome!" one of them said when she saw us. She was petite and tan, with short-cropped salt-and-pepper hair and wide-spaced blue eyes. "You young people must be some of our new dinner companions."

"Yes, we must," Alan said with a smile as he pulled out a chair for Bess. "I'm Alan, and these are my friends Bess, George, and Nancy." He pointed to each of us in turn.

"Lovely to meet you," the second woman spoke up.

She was taller and a little older than the first, with a graying blond bun and a bright smile. "I'm Alice, and these are my friends Babs and Coral."

"You can call us the ABCs," Coral spoke up with a titter. She was pleasantly plump and grandmotherly, with wire-rimmed glasses perched on her nose. "Get it? The ABCs—Alice, Babs, Coral."

"Nice to meet you," I said as I sat down between George and Babs.

"Yeah." George reached for her water glass. "I didn't realize we'd be sitting with other people."

Babs chuckled. "This must be your first cruise, then?"

"Yes, it is," Bess said. "And please don't be offended by what George said. She just meant—"

"It's all right, dear." Babs waved one wrinkled hand dismissively. "If it's your first time, a lot of things must seem rather strange."

Alice nodded. "But don't worry," she added. "The three of us are experienced cruisers. We'll show you the ropes."

"Really?" Alan said. "How many cruises have you been on?"

"Oh, dear, I'm not sure I can count that high anymore!" Coral giggled. "Let's just say it's enough that we should be able to answer any questions you may have. Right, girls?"

Alice nodded, but Babs was looking across the dining room. "I think our last two tablemates have arrived," she said.

I glanced over and saw the hostess approaching again. When I saw who was following her, I elbowed George. "Hey, it's the honeymooners!"

"Who?" Bess and Alan asked.

"Um, just someone we sort of met earlier," George told them.

By then the newcomers were at the table. Vince and Lacey both appeared to be in a much better mood than they had been the last time we'd seen them. Lacey looked lovely in a soft blue gown, and Vince was handsomer than ever in his dinner jacket and tie.

Soon more introductions had been traded. "Honeymooners, eh?" Coral said, winking at the rest of us. "Don't worry, we won't mind if you need to kiss between courses."

Meanwhile Babs was leaning forward, peering at Lacey. "You look familiar, my dear," she said. "Doesn't she, girls?"

Alice glanced over. "Oh, yes!" she exclaimed. "You don't have a sister who works for Jubilee Cruise Lines, do you?"

Coral gasped. "You're right! Why, if Lacey had darker hair and blue eyes, she'd be the spitting image of that pretty young singer on our Caribbean cruise last year!"

Lacey looked taken aback. "Um, no, you must be mistaken. I don't have a sister."

Vince put a protective arm around her shoulders. "It's okay," he told her. Then he smiled at the ABCs. "She's a little shy. Always gets tongue-tied when someone mentions how beautiful she is, even though it happens all the time."

"Well, of course it must!" Babs exclaimed, while Coral tut-tutted pleasantly.

Lacey gave them a wan smile. "I only wish I *was* related to someone at Jubilee," she said softly. "Maybe then we'd be on one of their cruises right now, instead of taking a chance on this brand-new untested cruise line." She shivered. "I haven't felt right since Vince and I spotted that body earlier."

"Body?" Alice's eyes widened. "What body?"

"Didn't you hear what happened at the pool right before we set sail?" Vince asked.

Coral leaned forward. "No, but do tell!"

I traded a worried look with Bess and George as the honeymooners started describing what had happened. The cruise director might have smoothed things over earlier, but it seemed the gossip was still spreading.

Just then there was a clatter from the next table. I glanced over and saw that Tobias, the bratty kid from our hall, had just dropped an entire tray of rolls on the floor. His father was scolding him while his mother bent down to try to salvage the rolls. Several waiters were already making a beeline for the table.

"That kid causes a commotion everywhere he goes, doesn't he?" George said.

I nodded. I'd just noticed that Wendy the travel blogger was at the same table as Tobias. She'd traded in her casual granny dress for a pink tulle vintage prom gown and a headband with a large plastic flower on it. Her laptop sat on the table beside her plate as she chattered nonstop at the man sitting next to her. I wasn't sure she'd even noticed the roll mishap.

"Whoa!" Alan exclaimed suddenly, staring off in a different direction. "Do you see who I see?"

As I glanced that way, a flash of color caught my eye. It was Mr. Hawaiian Shirt. He was sitting at another table with half a dozen other people. The others all appeared to be chatting and having a good time, but he was slumped in his chair, playing with his fork and looking fairly miserable.

George saw him too. "Hey! That mustache guy we met earlier didn't even bother to change clothes. So why do I have to dress up?" she complained.

"Huh?" Alan glanced at the man. "No, look over there. It's Merk the Jerk!"

He was pointing toward a different table. "Merk the Jerk," I echoed. "He's a stand-up comedian, right?"

"Yeah," George said. "His real name's Lou Merk. He's had a couple of TV specials and been in a few movies and some online stuff."

"I suppose he must be part of the shipboard entertainment." Babs peered in that direction. She sighed. "I'm just so disappointed that Brock Walker had to cancel!"

Just then a pretty young waitress hurried toward us. "Good evening," she said in a lilting Jamaican accent. "I'm Daisy, and I'll be your server tonight."

"Daisy?" George grinned. "What, are all the ship's employees required to have flower names or something?"

Daisy looked confused, though she smiled politely. "Can I start you off with some drinks?"

"Iris, remember?" George glanced around at Alan, Bess, and me. "That maid we saw earlier was named Iris, remember? Get it? Flower names?"

Bess ignored her. "I'd love an iced tea with lemon," she told Daisy.

As the others gave their drink orders, I noticed several men with video cameras hoisted on their shoulders entering the dining room. "What's going on over there?" I asked the waitress when she turned toward me.

She glanced over. "Let me get the maître d' so you can ask him."

Daisy walked to the front of the dining room and moments later returned with the maître d' in tow. His name tag read MR. PHILLIPS. I repeated my question.

"The camera crew?" he said. "They're just the ad people."

"Ad people?" Bess echoed.

"Didn't you get the insert in your info packages?" Mr. Phillips looked troubled. "It should have been covered in there."

Vince glanced at his wife. "We got the insert."

"So did we," Coral put in as her friends nodded.

"That explains it," Alan said. "See, we just won this cruise last week in an online contest. We didn't have time to get any info packs in the mail or anything."

Mr. Phillips nodded and explained, "The company hired the crew to do some candid filming during this inaugural cruise—just happy guests enjoying themselves, things like that. The footage will be used for future web ads and such."

"We could be in ads?" George sounded interested. "Cool."

"I do hope you won't mind being filmed," he continued. "But of course anyone who doesn't wish to take part should inform a member of the cruise staff as soon as possible." Mr. Phillips excused himself and returned to his post.

As Daisy finished taking our order and hurried off, I glanced again at the camera crew. When had they started filming? Could they have captured any footage earlier in the day that might help with the case? I made a mental note to try to track them down later.

"That was delicious." Bess pushed her chair back from the table about half an hour later. "If you'll all excuse me, I need to go powder my nose."

Yeah, Bess actually says things like that. Without irony, even. What can I say? It works for her.

"I'll come with you," I said quickly, dropping my cloth napkin beside my plate. "Uh, for the nose powdering, that is."

"Me too." George got up and followed us.

Soon we were in the ladies' lounge. It was just as opulent as the dining room—plush carpeting, chandeliers, a wall of mirrors with delicate upholstered stools in front of them, the works. But I barely spared a glance for any of it.

"Is anyone else in here?" I asked, peeking under the stall doors.

"Doesn't look like it." Bess sat down at the mirror and pulled a compact out of her purse. "Why? Do you have any new theories?"

"Not really." I quickly told her and George my idea about talking to the camera crew. "You never know," I said. "Maybe they caught someone carrying that mannequin around or something."

"Anything's possible." George sounded dubious. She was prowling back and forth across the lounge area, tugging at her dress as if it was choking her. "I guess this means you've decided there really is a mystery, huh?"

"It's sure looking that way." I glanced around again, making doubly sure we were alone. "And that's not all—I think someone's onto us."

Bess stopped applying powder to her already flawless skin and glanced at me in the mirror. "Onto us? What do you mean?"

"Something happened right before dinner," I began. "I've been dying to tell you, but with Alan around . . ." I went on to tell them about the note in my suitcase.

By the time I finished, Bess's eyes were wide and worried. "That really sounds like someone was threatening you!"

"Don't sound so shocked," George told her. "It's not like Nancy's never been threatened before. It kind of goes with the territory."

"Maybe," I agreed. "But nobody's supposed to

know why I'm really here, remember? So who could have done it?"

Before my friends could answer, the door swung open. Two giggling preteen girls rushed in with their middle-aged moms right behind them. Bess smiled politely, then stood up.

"We should get back to the table," she said, dropping her makeup back in her purse. "We don't want Alan to worry."

I was disappointed. My friends are always good at helping me figure things out, and I really wanted to talk about possible motives and suspects. But another woman was already coming in, and I realized our private moment was over.

"Let's go," I agreed with a sigh.

The bathroom was located in a hallway between the dining room and the stairwell. As we headed toward the former, we passed a door marked EMPLOYEES ONLY. It was standing slightly ajar, and I could hear angry voices coming from inside.

I paused, a little surprised. All the ship's employees

seemed to make a point of staying polite and cheerful anywhere passengers might hear. But whatever was going on just inside that door sounded anything but polite or cheerful. Most of it was too muffled to make out, though it sounded like two men arguing. Then one of them raised his voice.

"Drop it, John!" he said sharply. "Or I'll make sure you never make it to Anchorage!"

My eyes widened. That sounded pretty ominous.

"Hey," I called to my friends, who were a few steps ahead. "Hang on, I want to—"

"Ladies!" A loud, jovial voice interrupted me. Turning, I saw Marcelo, Becca's boss, hurrying up behind me, a broad smile on his handsome face. "I hope you're not lost. Can I have the honor of accompanying you back to the dining room?"

"Sure," Bess said with a smile.

I glanced helplessly at the door. But it was too late. The voices had stopped, so I had little choice but to allow the cruise director to sweep us all back into the dining room.

CHAPTER FIVE

Dangerous Games

"YOU'RE UP EARLY," I SAID AS I WALKED into the main room of the suite the next morning.

Bess glanced up with a smile. She was sitting at the glass-topped coffee table, stirring milk into a steaming mug of tea.

"You too," she said. "Luckily, Max the butler gets up even earlier. He brought us these." She waved a hand at the platter of bagels, doughnuts, and other pastries on the table in front of her.

"Great." I grabbed a glazed doughnut and took a bite. Then I wandered toward the balcony. The glass doors were open, offering a spectacular view of the shoreline we were passing as the ship made its way from Vancouver to our first shore stop in Ketchikan. Low hills draped in thick forests of pine and spruce tumbled to meet the sparkling deep-blue water, while in the distance, snow-capped peaks rose to meet the sky.

"Nice scenery, huh?" Bess said. "I could stare at that view all day."

I shot her a rueful look. "Me too. Unfortunately we don't have time," I said. "Have you seen George yet?"

Bess snorted. "What do you think? She's not exactly a morning person, remember?"

I grinned. "Understatement of the year. What about Alan?"

"Haven't seen him yet either. I guess he's still asleep."

"Good. Let's get George and get out of here before he wakes up," I said. "This could be our best chance to talk freely."

Shooting one last glance at the scenery, I turned and led the way toward the bedrooms. We tiptoed past

Alan's door. The sound of loud snoring was coming from inside.

Even louder snoring was coming from George's room. We let ourselves in. She was curled up on her side, with her back to us.

Bess leaned over and poked her cousin in the shoulder. "Rise and shine," she whispered loudly.

There was no response. I grabbed George's foot and tickled it. She shot up into a sitting position.

"Hey!" she blurted out.

"Shh!" Bess and I hissed.

George blinked stupidly for a moment, then glared at us. "What time is it?" she mumbled, making a move to lie down again.

But Bess was too fast for her. Grabbing her cousin's arm, she gave a yank that almost pulled her out of bed. "Get up," she ordered. "We need to get out of here before Alan wakes up. Nancy wants to talk."

It took a little more persuading, but finally we got her up. Leaving her to get dressed, Bess and I returned to the main room. I quickly gulped down some coffee while she scribbled a note for Alan.

"I'm telling him we're checking out the spa facilities to see if we can get facials this morning," she told me. "That should sound girly enough that he won't want to join us."

"No. But he might wonder why *George* wanted to join us," I joked just as George emerged, yawning and tousled, with damp hair from the shower and dressed in shorts and a River Heights University T-shirt.

"Huh? What'd you say?" she demanded sleepily.

"Never mind. Let's get out of here." I grabbed a jelly doughnut, stuffed it in her hand, then aimed her toward the door.

When we emerged from the suite, the hallway was empty except for a maid sweeping nearby. It was Iris from the day before.

"Hi." I smiled at her as we passed. "Excuse us."

"Guess she must be assigned to Tobias's cabin, like Max is to ours," Bess whispered as we hurried around the corner.

"Yeah." I grimaced. "Poor thing."

I forgot about the maid as I led the way toward the elevators. "Where are we going?" George asked, sounding marginally more awake as she finished the last bite of doughnut and licked jelly and powdered sugar off her fingers.

"Becca's office," I replied. "I'm hoping it's still early enough to catch her there. I want to finish our talk and maybe get a look at that threatening e-mail she got before the cruise. I know it's a stretch, but I might be able to tell if it was written by the same person who left me that note yesterday."

But when we knocked on Becca's door, there was no answer. I texted her and got a reply back within a minute or two.

"Where is she?" Bess asked as I scanned the message.

"She's hosting some kind of VIP breakfast reception," I said with a sigh. "Says she'll be tied up for the next hour or two at least. Oh well."

"Does that mean I got up at the crack of dawn for nothing?" George complained.

I ignored that. "Let's go check out the pool," I

said. "Maybe we missed a clue yesterday."

But that was another dead end. When we reached the pool area, it was spotless. Any trace of "blood" was gone from the water, which sparkled like glass beneath the early morning sun. Every trash receptacle was empty and appeared to have been bleached clean. Even the pool chairs were arranged in perfect lines.

Bess glanced into the same trash bin where George and I had found that drink mix container. "If there were any clues, they've definitely been cleaned up by now," she commented. "The cleaning staff here mean business!"

"Yeah." My shoulders slumped as I considered what to do next. "Maybe we should try the kitchen. Last night I heard arguing. . . ."

I filled them in on that snippet of argument I'd overheard as we walked. George looked dubious.

"Do you really think some random squabble is part of our case?" she asked.

I shrugged. "Probably not. But you never know. We're not exactly swimming in useful clues right now, in case you haven't noticed."

The main dining room was hushed and empty as we passed. But we heard the sounds of activity coming from a door right across the hall.

"That's the café," Bess said. "It's where we're supposed to eat breakfast and lunch. Dinner, too, if we don't feel like being so formal."

"What?" George yelped. "You didn't tell me that before you forced me to dress up like I was entering some girly-girl beauty pageant."

"Give it a rest," I told her. "Wearing a dress for a couple of hours didn't kill you, did it?"

I glanced into the café, which in this case seemed to be short for cafeteria. The setting was much less formal than the dining room, with passengers choosing their food from a long buffet line, then finding seats wherever they pleased. There were quite a few early risers in there, helping themselves to eggs, Danish, or fruit salad. I even spotted Tobias's parents, though the little boy was nowhere in sight.

We continued past the door to the employees-only entrance. As soon as we pushed it open, a cacophony of sounds and smells struck us—the sizzle of butter, the smell of bacon and eggs, the shouts of a dozen or more kitchen workers asking for more pancake batter or whatever. The hustle and bustle was a stark contrast to the serene peace of most of the ship.

"Now what?" George murmured in my ear. "Someone's going to notice us and kick us out soon."

I hardly heard her. I'd just spotted a familiar face. It was Mr. Hawaiian Shirt. Today's shirt bore a different raucous pattern from yesterday's, but otherwise he looked exactly the same. He was leaning against a stainless-steel countertop, stroking his mustache with one finger as he talked to a couple of young kitchen workers washing dishes nearby.

That was kind of weird. The first time we'd encountered him, he'd acted as if he didn't know his way around the ship. And last night he'd been sitting in the dining room like just any other guest. Could he actually be some kind of supervisor or something? He didn't exactly dress like the rest of the crew, but years of amateur sleuthing had taught me to assume nothing.

"Excuse me," I said, stepping over to him. "Do you work here?"

He blinked at me. "Oh, hello again," he said. "No, I don't work here. I just came back here to thank these hardworking people for their efforts and let them know it's appreciated by someone." He waved one meaty hand to indicate the kitchen staff, though the workers nearby had turned away and seemed to be pointedly ignoring him. "Now if you'll excuse me, I need some coffee."

Pushing past us, he hurried out of the kitchen. Bess stared after him.

"That was kind of a strange answer," she said.

George shrugged. "He seems like kind of a strange guy."

I tapped the nearest worker on the shoulder. "Hi," I said. "I don't mean to bother you, but I wonder if I could ask you a few questions."

The worker, a short, swarthy man with intelligent dark eyes, shrugged. "I'm sorry, miss," he said with a shy smile. "Guests should not be back here."

"I know. This'll just take a moment." I made my

smile as ingratiating as possible. "I was just wondering if there's been any trouble around here lately. In the kitchen, I mean. Anybody not getting along?"

"I would hope not," the worker responded. "If anything is upsetting you, however, the cruise staff is always available for complaints." He picked up a stack of dripping pans. "If you'll excuse me, I have to get back to work."

He hurried off before I could respond. I frowned, glancing around for another victim. At that moment the door swung open behind us.

"This way, kids!" a cheerful voice sang out. "Next I'm going to show you where all the food on the ship is prepared! If you're good, you might even get some samples!"

"Yay, samples!" several childish voices cheered.

"Good," another kid said. "I'm starved."

That last voice sounded cranky. And familiar. Turning, I saw that a whole group of kids had just entered the kitchen, led by the youth activities coordinator Becca had pointed out to Tobias's family yesterday.

And speaking of Tobias . . .

"This is boring," Tobias went on, scowling at the coordinator. "When are you going to show us something cool?"

The coordinator's smile barely wavered. "Now, now, Tobias," he began. "The tour's barely started. Just give it a chance, and I'm sure you—" He cut himself off as he noticed my friends and me. "Oh, hello," he said, hurrying over. His name tag identified him as Hiro. "You must be lost. Are you looking for the café?"

"No, we were just looking around," I said. "Thanks."

Hiro looked uncertain. "Um, passengers really shouldn't be back here."

"Why not?" George pointed at the kids. "They're passengers, right?"

"Yes," Hiro said. "But they're only here as part of the exclusive backstage tour of the ship."

"We're going to see everything!" a little girl spoke up eagerly. "Even the engine!"

Hiro smiled at her. "That's right, Maria," he said. Then he turned back to us. "There's a similar tour for adults—I think it's the day after tomorrow. If you're interested, all you have to do is let someone from the cruise staff know."

"Okay, maybe we will," Bess said. "Come on, girls, let's move on."

George and I followed her into the hall. "Okay, smelling all that food cooking made me hungry," George said. "What say we hit up that café? I'm not much good at sleuthing on an empty stomach."

"Take it easy, George," I said. "Just because it's all-you-can-eat, that doesn't mean you have to try to eat it all."

George looked up from her fourth helping of scrambled eggs. Bess and I had finished eating a good twenty minutes ago, but George seemed to be a bottomless pit.

"I'm almost done," she mumbled through a mouthful of toast.

Bess checked her watch. "I should check in with Alan," she says. "I just realized it's been, like, an hour and a half since we left the suite. He's probably wondering where we are." She pulled out her phone. "I'm surprised he hasn't been calling or texting me."

"Maybe he's still asleep," I suggested.

"Maybe." Bess texted him. A moment later her phone buzzed. "Nope, he's up," she reported a moment later. "He just texted me back."

By the time George finished her eggs, Bess had arranged to meet Alan on the Anchorage Action deck.

When we got there, Alan was waiting for us outside an Alaskan-themed snack bar. "Good morning, ladies," he sang out, stooping to plant a kiss on Bess's cheek. "You three were out and about early today!"

"Sorry for abandoning you," Bess told him, slipping her hand into his. "I just couldn't wait to check out the spa. Did you have breakfast?"

"Yes, back at the suite," he replied, patting his belly. "I couldn't let all those pastries go to waste! But now I'm thinking I need to work some of it off before lunch. What do you say to a round of miniature golf?" He gestured to a sign nearby. "I'll buy a smoothie for anyone who can beat my score."

"Mini golf? I'm awesome at that!" George said. "You're on."

"Why don't you three go ahead?" I said. "I'm not really in the mood for mini golf. I might go check out the shops or something."

Actually, I was thinking that playing miniature golf was a waste of time when I could be investigating. If I could get away, I'd have some time to snoop around, maybe track down that camera crew and see if they'd let me look at their footage.

But Alan shook his head. "What, are you afraid I'll beat you?" he teased. "Come on, Nancy, you can't chicken out."

I forced a smile. "It's not that. . . ."

Just then a pair of small boys came charging at us from around the corner of the snack bar. "I win!" one of them shouted as both skidded to a halt.

A moment later several other kids appeared too. Finally Hiro arrived, breathless and dragging Tobias by one hand. "Wait up, kids!" he called as his charges swarmed the snack bar. "Everyone's got to sit quietly before anyone gets their snack, okay?" Finally noticing us standing there, he smiled. "Oh, hello," he said. "Can I help you folks find anything?"

"Nope, we're good, bro," Alan told him. "We're just on our way to play some mini golf."

"Wonderful!" Hiro beamed at us. "Our brand-new miniature golf course is fabulous. It features a rugged Alaska theme."

"Sounds cool, thanks." Alan glanced at me as Hiro disappeared into the snack bar. "So what do you say, Nancy? You're not seriously going to ditch us, are you?"

I shot my friends a look, then glanced back at Alan. Was that a hint of suspicion in his eyes?

"Um, okay," I said. "You talked me into it."

The mini-golf course was actually pretty cool. As Hiro had promised, it featured an Alaskan theme complete with fake glaciers, grinning totem poles, a life-size moose, and a roaring grizzly on its hind legs.

"This is awesome!" Alan exclaimed. "Who wants to go first?"

For a while we had the place to ourselves. Just as

Bess was lining up a shot at a waterfall with little fake salmon leaping out of the water, we heard voices coming our way.

"Check it out," George said. "It's that camera crew. They probably heard about my awesome swing and ran right up here to get it on film."

Two burly cameramen stepped onto the course, along with a skinny young man dressed in black jeans and a gray T-shirt. Several passengers trailed in behind them.

"This way, everyone!" the skinny guy called. "Grab some clubs and we'll get started."

"I can't believe I'm gonna be in pictures!" an old man with a ring of white hair around his bald head exclaimed with a grin. "I'm ready for my close-up!"

"Stop, Harold." The woman with him rolled her eyes, rearranging her sun hat atop her tidy red curls. "You're such a ham!"

I recognized them as part of that family reunion we'd seen at the beginning of the trip. The group had been hard to miss at dinner last night, taking up three tables all on their own.

The thin young man spotted my friends and me and hurried over. "Good morning," he said. "I'm Claude, the director of the film crew." He looked me up and down. "Did anyone ever tell you that hair of yours is totally cinematic?"

I touched my hair, feeling self-conscious. "Um, I don't think so."

Claude glanced at the cameramen, who were already filming various parts of the mini-golf course. Establishing shots, I guessed.

"Baraz, get over here!" Claude barked. "I want to get this girl on film."

One of the camera operators, a man with a buzz cut, stepped toward us. "Sure, boss," he said, pointing his camera at me.

"No, not there—we need a better background." Claude glanced around, tapping his chin. "Something to set off that hair, that all-American complexion . . ."

"How about the moose?" Alan suggested. "That might look cool."

"Perfect!" The director clapped his hands. "The strawberry blond should really pop against the dark-brown fur."

I stepped toward the moose. Everyone was staring at me. Well, almost everyone. Bess and Alan seemed to have taken the distraction as an opportunity for a romantic moment. They were standing close together by the moose's side, laughing and talking softly while holding hands. But everyone else? Staring. At me.

"Is this okay?" I asked, striking a golf stance with my club near the moose obstacle.

"Closer," the director ordered. "We need to get all of the moose in frame."

I took a step back, glancing up at the moose's head looming above me. "Okay, now what?"

"Just forget that we're here," the director said. "Pretend you're just playing golf. Laugh and toss your hair and act normally."

I didn't bother to point out that I wouldn't be acting normally if I started tossing my hair around while I was playing mini golf. I quickly lined up my shot on the green, aiming for the hole directly underneath the towering moose.

Just as I was about to swing, I sensed something— movement right above me. Acting on instinct, I dropped my club and jumped back.

A split second later, one of the fake moose's huge antlers came crashing down—right where I'd just been standing.

CHAPTER SIX

❧

Animal Instincts

"NANCY!" BESS CRIED. "ARE YOU OKAY?"

"Yes. I mean no." I glanced down at my left arm, realizing that it was hurting. There was a trickle of blood on my forearm. "I mean, um, sort of."

By now George, Claude, and various others had reached me too. "Stand back, please!" Claude ordered. "She is injured!"

"Oh, dear!" one of the older ladies watching exclaimed.

"Shall we call the medic?" the old man called out.

"Of course we should, Harold!" his wife said. "Don't be such an old fool!"

Just then a young man in a Superstar uniform elbowed his way to the front of the crowd. It was Mike, the employee who'd helped us pick out our clubs. Hiro the youth coordinator was right behind him.

"What happened?" Mike asked. "You're bleeding."

"I'll call a medic." Hiro whipped out a cell phone.

"No, I'm okay." I took a deep breath, willing my heartbeat to return to normal. Then I glanced at my arm. "It's just a scrape—see? The edge of the antler must've caught me on its way down."

George frowned and glanced at the moose. "How'd that happen, anyway?" she wondered. Grabbing the moose's nose, she swung her leg up onto its knee and started climbing.

"Miss! Get down from here!" Mike warned. "Please, the medic will be here shortly."

"I told you, I'm fine," I insisted. "I don't need a medic."

George let out a cry. "Check this out!" she exclaimed. She'd climbed higher and was straddling the moose's neck by now. "It looks like someone loosened the screws that were holding that antler in place. All it would take is for someone to touch the moose, and *bam*! Down it would come."

Bess went white. "Oh no!" she cried. "It was me! I leaned back against the moose's side to get a better view of Nancy. It's all my fault!"

"Don't be silly." I grabbed her hand and squeezed it. "You had no way of knowing those screws were loose. Anyway, I'm fine."

Mike looked troubled. "This mini-golf course is brand-new," he said. "Someone must have forgotten to tighten those screws when they were putting everything together during setup."

Hiro bit his lip and clapped his hands sharply. "Please step away from the obstacles, everyone!" he called out. "We'll have to check them all for safety before the course can reopen. This was just an unfortunate accident, but we're taking care of it."

An accident? I wasn't so sure. From what I could tell, it seemed to fit the pattern of sabotage so far.

And I'm a target again, a little voice in my head added.

I shook off the thought. Accident or not, there was

no way the saboteur could have known I'd be the one standing beneath the moose. Was there?

Suddenly nervous, I glanced around. Two more employees had appeared and were busy herding Harold, his wife, and the other onlookers over toward the snack bar. Bess still looked distraught as she stared at my arm. Alan was next to her, murmuring into her ear. Most of the others were watching George climb down from the moose, including one of the cameramen, who was filming it.

My eyes widened as I remembered the cameras. The whole incident had been caught on tape! This could be the break we needed.

I glanced around. "Where's the other camera guy— Baraz?" I asked Claude. "We should look at the footage he got and see if we can tell what happened."

Claude glanced around too. "Looks like Baraz has disappeared." He frowned and muttered, "Again."

The other cameraman heard us and stepped forward. "I might have something," he offered. "The moose was in the background of what I was filming. See?"

He held out the camera so Claude and I could see its little playback screen. George, Bess, Alan, Mike, and Hiro huddled behind me, peering over my shoulders.

The playback focused on Bess and Alan. It was obvious that the cameraman had been going for a cute, romantic human interest scene of the two of them. They were standing to one side of the moose, laughing and flirting. I was barely visible in one corner, first standing there stiffly, then shuffling closer to the moose and lining up my shot.

"No!" Bess exclaimed as she watched Alan put his arm around her on the monitor, the two of them leaning back against the moose's furry side to watch my shot. "See? It really was my fault!"

"Our fault." Alan glanced at me. "We're so sorry, Nancy."

I waved him off, focusing on the monitor. "Can you play it back again?" I asked the camera operator.

But it was no use. The accident was visible in the background, but it was a pretty awkward angle, and we couldn't see much more than we already knew. The only thing the footage confirmed was that nobody else had been close enough to tamper with the moose.

As the second playback ended, my phone buzzed. I glanced at it and saw a text from Becca: SOMETHING ELSE JUST HAPPENED, she wrote. GOING 2 CHECK IT OUT. WILL UPDATE SOON.

The medic, a brisk woman in her thirties, appeared at that moment. "Step aside, please," she ordered. "Let's have a look."

She was still examining my arm when Becca rushed in, breathless and pink-cheeked. "Nancy!" she exclaimed when she saw me.

I smiled weakly as we both realized at the same time that I was the "something else" she'd just texted me about. One of the employees must have called her.

"I'm okay," I told her. I waved a hand at the medic. "This is just a precaution."

Becca nodded, though she didn't seem to be focused on me anymore. She was staring at Hiro, who was kneeling down to examine the fallen antler. There was a strange expression on Becca's face, one I couldn't quite figure out. What did that mean?

Before I could pull her aside to ask, Marcelo arrived on the scene. "Well, now," he exclaimed in his jovial voice. "What do we have here? Attacking mooses? Or is it meeses?" He chuckled. "I can never remember which it is." He came over and put a hand on my shoulder. "How is she, doc?" he asked the medic.

"She'll be fine," the woman replied. "But I'd better take her to the clinic and clean that scrape."

"It's okay," I said. "I have a Band-Aid back in the suite."

Just then Tobias stomped in, pushing past an employee who tried to stop him. "Hey!" he shouted. "When's the stupid tour going to start again?"

Hiro looked startled, as if he'd just remembered what he was supposed to be doing. "Sorry, Tobias," he said. "I'll be right there."

Tobias snorted and turned away. "Not that I care," he announced to no one in particular. "So far it's so boring that I might as well be sitting in my room staring at the wall."

Hiro shot Becca a nervous glance, then hurried after the boy. Suddenly Becca's strange look earlier made more sense. I guessed that as assistant cruise director, she was probably Hiro's direct supervisor. He had to feel embarrassed about getting caught abandoning his young charges, even given the unusual circumstances.

"You'll like the next part, Tobias," Hiro called out. "We're going to meet Captain Peterson and see all the computers and other high-tech stuff in the control room. Won't that be cool? I heard you're a real computer whiz. . . ."

His voice faded as he disappeared around the corner. Meanwhile the medic poked me in the shoulder. "Come," she said. "We're going to the clinic. No arguing."

Ten minutes later I was sitting on a cold plastic chair in a small but well-stocked medical clinic near the center of the ship while a nurse put a Band-Aid over my scrape. The medic was at a desk nearby, scribbling notes on some paperwork.

"Can I go now?" I called to her.

She glanced up and opened her mouth to answer. At that moment the door flew open and Wendy the blogger rushed in.

"Oh my gosh!" she cried when she spotted me. "Are you okay, Nancy? I just heard what happened!"

"News travels fast around here," I said.

The nurse was already bustling forward. "I'm sorry," she said. "Patients only allowed in here."

"But I want to interview her for my blog!" Wendy protested.

"You heard her. Out," the medic said sternly. "You can visit with your friend once she's released."

I didn't bother to explain that Wendy and I weren't exactly friends. Frankly, I was surprised she'd remembered my name.

Maybe she should be a suspect, I thought. *It's odd how she keeps turning up right after bad stuff happens. And wouldn't covering a bunch of crazy cruise disasters be a big draw for her travel blog?*

I was afraid Wendy might be waiting for me when

the medic finally released me from the clinic. Instead I found my friends out in the hall.

"Oh, good," Alan joked when he saw the bandage on my arm. "We were afraid they'd have to amputate."

"Very funny," I said with a smile—and a flash of guilt for wishing he wasn't there. I really wanted to talk to Bess and George about my new Wendy theory.

But that didn't seem likely to happen anytime soon. It was lunchtime by now, and Alan dragged us off toward the café. "I've heard the buffet on this ship is spectacular," he said.

"It is," George told him. "At least breakfast was pretty amazing."

"Yeah, and George would know. She ate most of it." Bess glanced at her cousin. "I can't believe you're ready for lunch already. Do you have a tapeworm or something?"

George shrugged. "Must be the sea air."

When we entered the café, at least half the tables were already occupied. More people were in the buffet line, helping themselves to the mountains of food piled there.

I glanced around, spotting a few familiar faces in the crowd as my friends and I joined the line to grab trays. Vince and Lacey were huddled over a single plate of french fries. The ABCs were at a different table, chatting with some passengers I didn't recognize. Tobias and his parents had a table to themselves near the dessert section.

"Look, there's Merk the Jerk again!" Alan pointed toward the center of the room. "Think he'd give me an autograph?"

Without waiting for an answer, he rushed off toward the table where the comedian was sitting. Merk was talking loudly, though I couldn't make out what he was saying from that distance. Whatever it was must have been funny, though, since the crowd gathered around him was laughing. I noticed that Wendy the blogger was among that crowd. So were a couple of cameramen, who were filming the whole scene.

George was looking that way too. "There's a motive for you," she commented.

"Huh?" I glanced at her as I grabbed a tray.

"Merk," George said. "With Brock out of the picture, he's the headline entertainment on this cruise now. That's got to be a boost to his career, right? Especially if he's featured in all the ads and stuff." She gestured toward the cameramen.

Bess reached for a roll. "That's true," she said. "But what about the pool incident and the other trouble? He'd have no motive for that stuff."

"Or would he?" I said thoughtfully, jumping back again to my theory about Wendy the blogger. Could the same idea apply here? "If this cruise becomes notorious enough, everyone will want to hear about it. And one place they'll look is online video sites."

George nodded. "And voilà—there's Merk!" she said, pausing to grab a handful of potato chips off the buffet. "It kind of makes sense."

"Only kind of." Bess still looked dubious. "I mean, Merk might not be A-list. But would he really risk his whole reputation like that?"

I realized it was kind of unlikely. But there was no more time to discuss it. Alan was on his way back from Merk's table.

"I couldn't even get close enough to ask," he reported, leaning past us to pick up a sandwich, which he set on Bess's tray. "I'll have to try again later."

As we sat down and started eating, I was surprised to see the ship's captain making a beeline for our table. He was a handsome, broad-shouldered man of about fifty. I'd seen him from a distance, but hadn't met him yet.

"Good afternoon," he greeted us, his eyes flicking over the other three before settling on me. "I'm Captain Reece Peterson. I was hoping to find you here." His gaze wandered to the bandage on my forearm. "I heard about the—er—incident at the miniature golf course earlier."

"Yeah," George said. "Nancy almost got killed by that vicious moose. That's probably worth a free shore meal in Ketchikan at least, huh?"

Bess elbowed her cousin hard in the ribs. "She's just kidding," she told the captain with a smile. "Nancy's fine."

"Yeah," I added. "It's just a flesh wound."

I expected him to smile and move on. But he just

stood there for a moment, shifting his weight from one foot to the other. The expression on his tanned, chiseled face was troubled.

"Good, good," he said after an awkward delay. "Uh, Marcelo tells me there were several ship personnel on the scene assisting you when he arrived. Do you happen to recall who they were? We just want to, uh, commend them."

"Yoo-hoo! Captain Peterson!" Just then Coral hurried over, all smiles. "Are you getting acquainted with our lovely young first-time cruisers?"

The captain turned to smile and trade pleasantries with her, giving me the chance to shoot a perplexed glance at Bess and George. Why had the captain just asked me which employees had been present during my accident? Could he be worried that one of them was involved? Was it possible that he knew who I really was and why I was there? Becca claimed that she was the only one onboard who did. But what if Verity had filled him in without telling Becca?

By then Coral was moving on toward the buffet

line, saying something about testing out all the desserts. The captain turned back to me.

"About those employees, Miss Drew . . . ," he began.

I watched as Coral reached the dessert area, mostly as an excuse not to meet the captain's eye. So I was looking right at her when she reached for a pastry, let out a loud gasp—and then crumpled to the floor!

"Coral!" I blurted out, on my feet before I knew it.

Other people closer to her were exclaiming in alarm and rushing to help as well. I was halfway there when the screams started.

"What's going on?" George panted in my ear as she caught up to me. "Did Coral just faint?"

"I guess so. But what's going on there?" My gaze shot from the people kneeling beside Coral to the buffet, where several other passengers were peering at a tray piled high with pastries.

"Stop!" a man I didn't know cried as George and I came closer. "Stand back! There's a tarantula in the cream puffs!"

CHAPTER SEVEN

Unusual Suspects

I GASPED AS I SAW SOMETHING SCUTTLE over an éclair and disappear behind a pile of brownies. "Was that really . . . ," I began.

"A tarantula!" George finished. "Whoa!"

"Don't hurt her!" a voice rang out behind us, cutting through the clamor. "Please! She's friendly."

"Tobias!" Bess exclaimed. She and Alan had caught up by now. "What's he doing?"

We all watched as the kid pushed his way to the buffet. Standing on tiptoes to peer over the pastry tray, he leaned forward and scooped something up. When he turned around, we could all see a huge, hairy spider perched on his hand.

"Tobias!" His father had hurried forward by now as well. "Is that Hazel?"

"Hazel?" George echoed, raising one eyebrow.

"No wonder Coral fainted," I said, staring as the spider climbed slowly up Tobias's arm. Her black-and-orange body was thicker than his wrist. "Who wants to see something like *that* sitting on your dessert tray?"

Glancing at Coral, I saw that she was already sitting up with help from Captain Peterson and other bystanders, looking dazed but sheepish.

The captain cleared his throat and called for attention. "Let's all calm down, please," he said in a voice of authority. "Are you all right, ma'am?"

"Oh, yes, I think so." Coral was on her feet by now. "Though, silly me, I'm not entirely sure what just happened!"

"It's pretty clear what happened, I'm afraid," Tobias's father said grimly, grabbing his son by the shoulder. "Tobias must have sneaked his pet spider onboard, and then decided to cause a ruckus by dropping her in the food."

"Ow!" Tobias wriggled out of his father's grasp, the sudden motion almost causing the tarantula to lose its grip on his arm. Hazel gave a little jump, ending up clinging to Tobias's shirt. A couple of passengers nearby went pale and took a few steps backward.

"I always kind of wanted a pet tarantula," George commented to nobody in particular.

I looked at her. "Not helping," I said.

Meanwhile Tobias turned to glare at his father. "You're right, I did sneak Hazel onboard." His lower lip stuck out defiantly. "I needed *something* to keep me busy on this trip." He carefully stroked the tarantula's hairy back as she climbed up toward his shoulder. "But I *didn't* put her in the food. She could have been crushed!"

The boy's mother joined them, her face pale and angry. "Don't lie to us, Tobias," she said. "The evidence is right there on your shirt, remember?"

"I'm not lying!" Tobias glared at her, his eyes flashing

angrily. "The last time I saw Hazel she was in her cage in our stupid cabin. I told you, I'd never leave her where she could get hurt!"

"Hmm." His father didn't look convinced. "I think we'd better continue this discussion in our cabin. So sorry for the disruption, everyone." Stepping over to Coral, he put a hand on her arm. "Special apologies to you, ma'am. I hope you're okay."

"Oh, I'm just fine." Coral smiled as brightly as ever, though she still looked pale. Alice and Babs took her by the arms and led her toward their table.

Tobias was dragged off in the opposite direction by his parents, loudly proclaiming his innocence all the while. Captain Peterson watched them go, then squared his shoulders.

"All right, folks, show's over. Please go back to enjoying your meals." He glanced at several employees, who were already busy clearing away the trays where the tarantula had been. "Fresh desserts will be out shortly."

He strode off toward the exit, seeming to forget that

we hadn't finished our conversation. Good. I needed to talk to my friends about what had just happened.

"Wow, that was creepy, huh?" Alan commented, slinging an arm over Bess's shoulders.

Oops. I'd almost forgotten about him.

"Hey, Alan," I said as we walked back to our table. "Seeing that spider made me feel a little shaky. Would you mind grabbing me a soda? With extra ice?" I gestured toward the drink station at the far end of the line.

"Sure, Nancy. Be right back." He smiled at me.

"Isn't he sweet?" Bess gave a little wave as Alan loped off. "It's nice to spend time with a guy who's so nice and considerate to everyone."

"Yeah, whatever." I didn't want to waste time discussing Alan's virtues. "Listen, we need to talk."

George sat down and picked up her sandwich. "What's to talk about? This is one crazy incident that's no mystery."

"Agreed." Bess's eyes widened. "Actually, it might even solve another mystery. I bet that spider is how Tobias scared the maid yesterday! In the hallway, remember? He stuck something in his pocket—I bet it was Hazel."

"You're probably right." I sank into my chair, thinking hard. "But listen, maybe we shouldn't be so quick to assume this has nothing to do with the other incidents."

George let out a snort. "What, do you think Tobias is the one who's been sabotaging the cruise?"

"Maybe," I said. "Think about it. Hiro mentioned earlier that Tobias is good with computers."

"He did?" Bess blinked at me.

I nodded. "When he was chasing him out of the mini-golf place earlier. Anyway, if it's true—like, if Tobias is really some kind of computer genius—he could have sent those e-mails to Becca and Brock. Maybe he was trying to get the whole cruise shut down so he could go to that amusement park instead. It's obvious he wants to be anywhere else but here."

"They wouldn't shut down a cruise over a couple of e-mails," George said.

I shrugged. "Tobias is just a kid. He wouldn't necessarily realize that. Anyway, that mannequin stunt was pretty childish, if you think about it. And Becca said the drink mix came from the kids' section, remember? Plus, Tobias was nearby during the moose incident this morning."

My friends traded a glance, looking skeptical. I couldn't really blame them.

"Okay, so it's a little far-fetched," I said. "So are all our other theories so far."

"Incoming," George hissed, glancing over my shoulder.

Alan was hurrying toward us, holding my glass of soda. I sighed, then pasted on a smile. Further discussion would have to wait.

"Come on, dude." Vince the newlywed grinned as he hung at the edge of the pool, his hair slicked back. "We need one more guy for even teams."

Alan sat up straight on his lounge chair. It was an hour after lunch, and he'd insisted we all change into our bathing suits and get some sun. I was itching to get away and do some investigating, but I hadn't found the right excuse yet.

"Volleyball, huh?" Alan said, glancing from Vince to the four other guys of various ages out in the pool. "I'm not bad at that, if I do say so myself."

A few members of the film crew were nearby, getting shots of passengers enjoying the pool. One of the cameramen came closer, his lens trained on Alan and Vince. "Go on, man," he called. "This could be great stuff for the ads."

Another cameraman was filming the guys in the pool. He glanced over his shoulder at Alan. "You guys'll be Superstar superstars," he joked.

I peered at him over my sunglasses. It was Baraz, the one who'd disappeared so abruptly yesterday.

"Okay, how can I say no to that?" Alan peeled off his T-shirt and stood up, tugging up the waistband of his swim trunks.

"Have fun," Bess said, glancing up from her fashion magazine.

Alan grinned, dropped a quick kiss on top of her

head, then cannonballed into the pool to loud cheers from the other guys. I sat up, dropped the book I'd been pretending to read, and scooted my lounge chair a little closer to my friends. It was a gorgeous afternoon and the pool was busy, but none of the other sunbathers were close enough to overhear us.

"Okay, where were we?" I said briskly.

George looked up from her laptop with a smirk. "You were trying to convince us that an eight-year-old is some kind of criminal mastermind," she joked.

I smiled. "Okay, I already admitted that one's a little bit of a stretch," I reminded her. "So let's come up with some other ideas." I'd spent the past half hour stewing over the case while pretending to read my book, so I was ready. "I'm thinking we shouldn't focus too much on motives right now—it's just too random. Instead let's think about opportunity. Who could have done the things that have happened so far?"

"Just about anyone on the ship." George shrugged. "I mean, we're all stuck in this floating tin can together. Equal opportunity."

"Not really." Bess looked thoughtful. "There weren't that many people around the mini-golf place this morning. If the bolts on that antler were loose enough to let go just because Alan and I leaned back against the moose's side, it probably couldn't have been that way for long, right?"

"Good point." I thought back to the incident. "Actually, I did notice something weird right after it happened."

"What? Tobias sneaking around with a monkey wrench?" George teased.

"No. It was when Becca arrived on the scene."

Bess cocked an eyebrow. "Hang on, you're not suspecting *Becca*, are you?"

I shook my head. "It's just that I noticed her giving Hiro a really funny look when she spotted him there."

"Hiro? You mean that kiddie wrangler guy?" George tugged at the strap of her one-piece swimsuit. "Come to think of it, he totally encouraged us to check out the mini golf, remember?" She grinned. "Hey, while we're at it, playing mini golf was all Alan's idea. Maybe *he* did it!"

Bess gave her a sour look. "Very funny." Then she glanced back at me. "I do remember Hiro being nearby with the kids when we got there. I'm not sure he could've sneaked away from them long enough to loosen the bolts, but I guess you never know."

I nodded. "I'll have to ask Becca about him when I get a chance. Anybody else we should think about?"

"What about *him*?" George was staring at the action out in the pool.

I followed her gaze. The water volleyball game was in full swing. As Vince spiked the ball over the net, one of the cameramen leaned in to capture the action shot.

"Baraz," I murmured thoughtfully, watching him. "Yeah, that was kind of weird how he disappeared right after the accident."

"And that director made it sound like it wasn't the first time," George recalled. "What if he was off tossing his monkey wrench overboard?"

"Anything's possible. But why? What's his motive?" I sighed, realizing that sentiment was becoming a refrain for this case. I realized something else. "It's also possible that the moose thing was just an accident. Like someone said, it's a brand-new ship. We might have been the very first ones to test out the course. Maybe the screws didn't get tightened enough and they just let go."

"That's probably at least as likely as some eight-year-old supervillain being strong enough to loosen a bunch of bolts," George said. "Especially when he was supposed to be on a tour with a bunch of other kids and Mr. Nanny at the same time."

"True. But I'm not ready to totally cross Tobias off the list yet, given what just happened at lunch. Anyway, maybe we should move on to something we *know* wasn't an accident—namely the mannequin stunt." I glanced at a lounge chair across the pool, where Lacey was lying on her stomach, watching her new husband and the others. "I think I'll go ask Lacey a few questions about what she saw."

I hurried over to her. She squinted up at me when I arrived. "Hi," Lacey said. "It's Nancy, right?" She smiled apologetically. "Sorry, there are so many new names to remember!"

"Yeah, it's Nancy. Hi, Lacey." I perched on Vince's empty chair beside hers. "Listen, I was just thinking about what happened yesterday. It kind of gave me the creeps. Maybe we should notify the police. Were you the first person to see that mannequin in the pool?"

"I guess so." Lacey visibly shuddered. "Vince was with me, of course, but he didn't notice it at first. It was so horrible! I couldn't help screaming my head off, even though I felt like an idiot afterward."

"Nobody thinks you're an idiot," I said with a smile. "Did you notice anyone else near the pool at the time? Any kids, maybe?"

Lacey didn't seem to hear me. She was staring out at the pool toward the spot where the mannequin had been floating. "I've had the strangest feeling ever since then," she said softly, seeming to speak more to herself than to me. "It's like I'm waiting for the next terrible thing to happen." She shuddered again. "I'm really beginning to think this whole cruise is cursed!"

CHAPTER EIGHT

Following Leads

I YAWNED AS I QUIETLY PULLED THE SUITE door shut behind me. The early wake-up call I'd requested had come right on time, though Max had seemed as chipper and wide awake as ever when he'd knocked on my door. Meanwhile all I'd wanted to do was crawl back into bed, let my head sink into my special buckwheat pillow, and go back to sleep for another hour or two.

But I hadn't. The ship would be arriving in Ketchikan in a few hours, and I wanted to get some investigating done before then. Or before something else happened.

Thinking back on Lacey's gloomy prediction yesterday, I couldn't help shivering a little myself.

It's a good thing she doesn't know about the rest of the bad stuff that's happened, I thought as I hurried through the silent hallways. *If the passengers find out about all that, it could be a disaster for this ship. Not to mention Superstar Cruises.*

I quickly banished the thought. I was going to make sure that didn't happen. First on the agenda? Talking to Becca. I wanted to ask her about Hiro, and maybe take a look at that threatening e-mail.

I'd already texted Becca to check that she was awake—and alone. When I arrived at her office, she was bent over her laptop at the desk again.

"Hi, Nancy," she said, sounding tired as she glanced up. "Give me some good news. Did you figure out what's going on around here?"

"We're working on it," I said, leaning against the doorframe. "I just need to ask you . . ."

I let my voice trail off as I heard footsteps hurrying along the hallway. Glancing out, I saw a familiar figure clicking toward me on high-heeled navy pumps.

"Tatjana!" Becca said in surprise as the woman brushed past me into the office. "What's wrong?"

"Big problems," Tatjana barked out.

Becca sat up straight, weariness replaced by wariness. "Oh, no. What now?"

"We're getting tons of reports from levels five through seven," Tatjana replied. "The passengers have been calling since midnight to complain that their temperature control systems are going haywire. Half the cabins are boiling hot, and the other half are freezing."

"I'd better go deal with this." Becca sounded dismayed. She headed for the door, pausing beside me as if belatedly remembering that I was there. "Sorry, Nancy," she added. "Talk later?"

"Sure." I turned to follow her out of the room, only to find Tatjana staring at me. Again.

"May I help you?" she asked. "I report directly to Becca. I'm sure I could answer whatever questions you have for her."

"That's okay." I pasted on a bright smile. "It's nothing important."

As soon as I was safely out of sight around the corner, my smile faded and I collapsed against the wall. Unless I missed my guess, those haywire heating systems were no accident. Our saboteur had struck again—and the voyage was just getting started. I was no closer to guessing his or her identity.

Chewing my lip, I mentally ran through my suspect list. But it was pathetically short, and some of the people on it were laughable. An eight-year-old boy? Really? Was I that desperate?

I wandered up the stairs to the promenade deck, where many of the ship's shops were located. Pausing in front of a clothing store, where several expressionless mannequins posed in the window like giant creepy dolls, I flashed back to the pool incident. Unbidden, a chilling question popped into my head: *That body was fake, but what if the next one's real?*

My mind jumped to that ominous note in my suitcase, and then to the moose antler crashing down inches from me. The latter could be a random accident, maybe, but not the former. Was someone targeting *me* as well as the ship? But how had they found out about me?

The promenade deck was almost deserted at that hour, since most of the shops were still closed. I wandered past one darkened storefront after another as I thought over the suspect list. Hiro was a big question mark. Yes, he'd been around for the moose incident—and the pool one too, come to think of it. And being an employee, he'd have easy access to the mannequins and such, as well as to the heating and cooling system. But what was his motive? Could there be a clue in that weird look Becca had given him? I would have to wait until I talked to her to find out.

Then there was the disappearing cameraman, Baraz. He'd been nearby during the moose incident too. The other members of the camera crew? I had no idea. But I guessed that the crew had nearly unlimited access to the ship. Probably even the "backstage" parts, which meant he could also be involved in that heated argument I'd overheard.

And what about Wendy the blogger? I paused, noticing the ship's Internet café right across the concourse. Some of her behavior had been sort of suspicious, and she seemed pretty serious about her blog. Was that enough of a motive for her to want to ruin the cruise?

There were lights on in the Internet café, so I walked over and peered in the window, wondering if she could be in there right now, sending off her latest entry. Instead I saw an even more familiar face bent over one of the terminals.

"George!" I called, hurrying inside. "What are you doing up at this hour?"

She glanced up at me with a yawn. "Trust me, it wasn't my idea," she said, sounding cranky. "Alan woke me up with all his crashing around in the bathroom. Remind me again why we let him come?"

I ignored that. "I'm glad you're here," I said. "Feel like taking a peek at our favorite travel blogger's work?"

"You mean Wendy the weirdo? Sure." George's fingers flew over the keyboard.

Within seconds, Wendy's Wanderings was up on the screen. The blog's top entry was titled "Terror on the High Seas."

"Uh-oh," I said, shoving George aside so I could perch on the chair with her. "That doesn't sound good. . . ."

I leaned forward to read. It turned out to be a funny entry about the tarantula incident. Wendy had even done some research, discovering that Tobias and his parents lived in Vancouver, which was why Hazel hadn't been confiscated by customs agents or noticed at all until yesterday. The boy had hidden the spider's cage in his suitcase and Hazel herself in his pocket as they boarded, then kept her presence a secret from his parents until she'd appeared on the buffet, telling them he'd left her with a school friend for safekeeping. The way Wendy told it, the whole thing came across as a humorous episode.

"She's actually not a bad writer," George said as she read.

"Yeah." I scrolled down, checking out the next latest few entries. There were about half a dozen so far about the cruise, mostly short ones describing the food, entertainment, and lodgings. But there was one more that caught my attention: "Blood (Sort of) in the Water."

"Hey, she wrote about the pool thing," George said as she spotted it too. "Wow, she even got a picture of the lifeguard dragging the mannequin out of the water!" She leaned closer, peering at the photo. "The blood looks a lot more lifelike in the picture."

I nodded as I scanned through the entry. This one read more like a news report, describing what had happened and saying that ship employees claimed it was a prank. I winced when I read the last few lines: *But seeing a dead body in the pool—even a fake one—isn't the best way to start a relaxing cruise to glacier country. More like an epic fail, actually. Is it enough to sink this brand-new cruise line before it leaves the harbor? Only time will tell....*

George pointed to the bottom of the entry. "She got a bunch of comments on this one," she said. "That means a lot of people read it."

"That could be our motive right there. It's pretty suspicious that she happened to be close enough to get photos before they shooed everyone away."

George scrolled back up. "Let's see if we can find out more about our happy blogger. . . ."

But the "About Me" section of the blog didn't have much information. It just gave Wendy's name and age and mentioned that she lived in Seattle when she wasn't "traveling the world in search of the next adventure."

"Should I run a web search, see if I can find out more about her?" George suggested.

I was about to tell her to go ahead when my phone buzzed. It was Bess.

"Are you with George? We're saving seats for you two at breakfast," she said. In the background, I could hear Alan chatting with someone, though I couldn't tell who. "You'd better hurry up—we don't have much time to eat before we dock in Ketchikan."

"Drat," I muttered as I hung up. "I guess more research will have to wait."

We found Bess and Alan sitting with Vince and Lacey in the café. "There you are!" Vince greeted us with a smile. "Your friends were worried that you'd fallen overboard or something."

"Nothing that drastic, just taking a walk." I sat down and smiled politely at Vince and Lacey. "So are you guys looking forward to Ketchikan?"

Lacey glanced up from buttering her toast. "Oh, we're not going ashore," she said. "We decided to skip Ketchikan and stay on the ship."

"Really? Why?" George asked.

"I'm not really in the mood for sightseeing," Lacey said softly, shooting a look at her husband.

Vince explained, "She's still a little shaken up over what happened the other day. We figured we'd just hang out on the ship, have a quiet day on our own while everyone else is away."

I was a little surprised, since this was Alaska, after all. But . . . this was their honeymoon, and it was no wonder that the brand-new husband and wife might want to spend some private time together rather than surrounded by a bunch of strangers with nowhere to really get away. I was feeling some of that myself, actually.

Maybe I should stay on the ship too, I thought as I

chewed the bagel I'd grabbed from the buffet. *That would give me a chance to investigate without having to dodge Alan or make small talk with random other passengers or whatever. I might even find a moment to sit down with Becca and really talk about the case without being interrupted every two seconds.*

It was a tempting thought. But I wasn't sure it was worth the trouble. How would I explain to Alan why I wasn't going ashore? It was probably too late to fake an illness. Besides, most of the trouble so far had been very public. If the saboteur was going to strike again, it seemed more likely to happen where the passengers *were* than where they weren't. In other words, if there was any action today. it was probably going to happen in Ketchikan, and I didn't want to miss it.

"Yo, Scott!" Alan shouted just then, jumping to his feet so fast he almost upended his orange juice. He waved his arms vigorously. "Over here, bro!"

I glanced over and saw the shore excursion specialist we'd met on the first day. He was carrying a clipboard and a stack of envelopes.

"Hi," he said when he reached our table. "Everyone ready for some big fun in Ketchikan today?" He shuffled through the envelopes. "Alan, I got your message. You four are signed up for the deluxe town tour, followed by the lumberjack show, and then a floatplane ride to the Misty Fjords."

"What?" George looked up from her french toast. "I mean, wait—what?"

I couldn't have said it better myself. "You signed us up for all that stuff?" I asked Alan. "When were you planning to fill us in?"

Alan grinned. "You're welcome," he said. "Some of these shore excursions fill up early, you know. You girls have been so busy running off getting facials and stuff that I was afraid we'd get shut out."

"Oh." I traded a look with George and Bess. Being stuck in a bunch of structured tours and activities wasn't exactly the Ketchikan experience I'd had in mind. How was I supposed to check out our suspects that way, unless they happened to have the exact same itinerary?

"It's okay," Bess said, giving Alan's shoulder a squeeze. "We appreciate it, Alan. It'll be fun. Right, girls?"

"I wanted to go kayaking," George grumbled. But seeing Bess's glare, she shrugged. "But whatever."

"Um, actually I was thinking it would be fun to just wander around town on our own," I said. "From the tour books in our suite, it looks like there's a ton to see and it's all pretty close together. But I don't mind doing that by myself if you guys want to do the other stuff."

Scott was still standing by, his hand holding a pen poised over his clipboard. "So that's down to three for the activities?" he asked.

"No!" Alan protested before I could respond. "Come on, Nancy. I put a lot of thought into these activities— I really think you'll enjoy them." He grinned. "And I won't take no for an answer!"

I hesitated, trying to figure out a way around this. But looking at Alan, I could tell it was no use. I pasted on a smile, though it felt a little weak around the edges.

"Okay," I told Scott. "Put us down for four."

CHAPTER NINE

Stalling Out

"THAT WAS COOL," BESS SAID. "I NEVER thought I'd see a bald eagle up close like that, let alone a whole bunch of them!"

"See?" Alan slipped an arm around her shoulders. "I told you guys this would be great."

I tucked my camera back in my pocket, squinting a little in the midday sunlight. It was a beautiful day with hardly a cloud in the sky, despite Ketchikan's nickname being the Rain Capital of Alaska.

"This way, people!" Scott called out. "That concludes the deluxe tour, so those of you who aren't signed up for anything else today are free to go shop, eat, or sightsee on your own. However, anyone who's signed up to see the world-famous Great Alaskan Lumberjack Show should stick around. It's just a short walk from here, so if you'll follow me . . ."

Most of us fell into step behind him, chattering about the things we'd seen over the past couple of hours. There were about a dozen people on the tour. Unfortunately, none of our suspects were among them. The only people we'd known before the tour started were the ABCs.

"I've heard this lumberjack show is a real hoot," Babs said, falling into step beside me.

I nodded and smiled, though I was feeling distracted. Yes, the tour had been fun. We'd taken a carriage ride through the picturesque town, visited a salmon hatchery, and then toured a place where people took care of injured bald eagles and other wildlife. All that had sidetracked me from the case for a while, but now I was getting restless.

When Babs turned to talk to Coral, I sidled away toward my friends. Bess and Alan were walking hand in hand, but George had slowed down to fiddle with her camera, so I was able to pull her aside.

"We're wasting time here," I whispered.

George glanced up. "What do you mean? Alan actually came through for once—that tour was cool."

"I know. But I was really hoping to get a chance to check out some of our suspects today, like Wendy or maybe Tobias."

"Okay, but how would you find those people even if we did get away?" George shrugged and glanced around. "Open your eyes. Ketchikan is a mob scene."

I saw her point. The *Arctic Star* wasn't the only cruise ship docked in Ketchikan at the moment. There were two other massive ships there, and their passengers were everywhere.

"Anyway," George went on with a grin, "I hear this lumberjack show is pretty fun. Let's check it out, and then maybe we can duck out of the fjord thing afterward, okay?"

I sighed. It would have to do. "Fine," I said. "Lumberjacks it is."

Soon we were all seated in the grandstand of the open-air arena where the lumberjack show would take place. My friends and I were at the end of a row about halfway back, with most of the seats nearby taken up by *Arctic Star* passengers. Scott was at the end of the aisle a couple of rows ahead of us.

"Relax, folks," he called out as he sat down. "The show's scheduled to start in about fifteen minutes."

"I wonder what all the other people from the ship did this morning," Alan said. "Scott said a bunch went kayaking or fishing. And some others did this tour where you go into the rain forest and do a zip-line thing. Maybe we should have tried that."

"Zip lining? No thank you." George shuddered. "We had, uh, a bad experience with a zip line once. Right, Nancy?"

I shot her a warning look. She was right—I'd had a pretty bad accident on a zip line in Costa Rica once because someone had sabotaged it to try to stop one of my investigations. Alan already knew I was an amateur detective, of course—pretty much everyone in River

Heights did. But I didn't particularly want to remind him about my little hobby. He came across as pretty goofy, but he wasn't stupid. What if he figured out what I was really doing on this cruise?

Luckily, though, Alan didn't seem to have caught the comment. "It's weird to think of a rain forest in Alaska, isn't it?" he mused. "I mean, when you think Alaska, you think snow and glaciers and stuff, not rain forest."

"Very educated comment, Mr. Environmental Studies Guy," George quipped.

Alan looked annoyed. "Hey, I may be an enviro student, but that doesn't mean I'm an expert on every environment on the planet, all right?"

"Look," Bess said, clearly trying to distract them from sniping at each other. "I think I see some other people from our ship coming in. Including our favorite arachnophile."

"Huh?" George glanced toward the entrance, then made a face. "Quick, everybody hide," she hissed. "It's Spider Boy!"

I looked too and saw Tobias entering the grandstand with his parents. For a second my instinct was the same as George's. But then I realized this might be my only chance today to do any investigating. Okay, so it involved our weakest suspect. Still . . .

"Hello!" I called to the family, standing up and waving. "There are some seats over here!"

Tobias's mother spotted me and waved back. Moments later they were making their way toward us.

George groaned softly. "Are you nuts?" she whispered. "That kid's scary enough even *without* easy access to axes and stuff."

But there wasn't time to say any more before Tobias pushed past us and flopped into an empty seat. "I hope the show starts soon," he said impatiently. "It's probably going to be the only interesting thing I get to do on this whole stupid cruise."

"Relax, son," his father said with a sigh. "It'll start soon."

"So what did you kids see in Ketchikan so far today?" his wife asked us.

The small talk continued from there. It turned out the family had spent the morning wandering around sightseeing on their own instead of joining any of the organized activities. I couldn't help wondering if that was because Tobias was being punished for the spider stunt. Had he confessed to planting Hazel on the buffet yet?

I cast around in my mind for a subtle way to ask. But Alan, of all people, beat me to it.

"Hey, buddy," he said with a grin, leaning toward Tobias. "Did you bring Hazel along to check out the show too?"

Tobias gave him a withering look. "What do *you* think, genius?" he snapped.

"Tobias! Manners!" his mother scolded. Then she smiled at Alan. "Sorry. He's a little touchy about Hazel right now."

"Yes, and he's not making it easy on himself." Tobias's father looked at his son sternly, though Tobias ignored him. "The ship is being nice about what happened, and Miss Coral has been especially gracious. But Tobias still won't admit to what he did."

His wife sighed. "It's just not like him," she murmured. "Tobias can be, er, difficult. But he's not normally a liar. I certainly hope this isn't a new phase. . . ."

"At least Hazel has been confined to her cage since yesterday," Tobias's father said, clearly trying to lighten the mood. "I'm sure everyone's glad about that—well, except maybe for Analyn."

"Analyn?" I echoed.

"She's the maid for our cabin," Tobias's mother explained with a rueful smile. "Lovely young girl from the Philippines. Poor thing—she probably wasn't expecting to see a tarantula sitting on the coffee table when she brought the clean towels in last night. Even one in a cage."

My friends chuckled, but I frowned slightly. "Wait," I said. "I thought the maid for your cabin was named Iris."

"They probably have more than one," Bess said. "Like us, remember? Our suite has Max plus the two maids."

"That's right, there are two cabin stewards for ours as well," Tobias's father said. "Analyn and a young man named John."

"Oh." Something about this was bothering me, though I wasn't sure what. "So the maid we saw, Iris—"

At that moment, Tobias leaped to his feet. "Hey! Look, there's seats right down in front!" he blurted out loudly, interrupting me. He stomped on my toes as he raced for the aisle. "Come on, let's go before someone takes them!"

"Sorry, sorry," his father said breathlessly as he and his wife followed.

"It's okay," Bess said. Then she turned and smiled sweetly at Alan. "We still have a few minutes before the show starts. Think I have time to go find a soda before that? I'm parched."

Alan jumped to his feet. "Stay here—I'll find you one."

George watched him hurry out, then turned to Bess. "How do you *do* that?"

Bess ignored her. "So what do you think?" she asked me. "Are you ready to cross our favorite spider wrangler off the suspect list?"

"I'm not sure," I said slowly. "On the one hand, it's

weird that he won't confess. It's not like he's shy about causing trouble most of the time."

"Good point," George put in. "If anything, you'd think he'd be bragging about it."

"On the other hand," I went on, "who else even knew that spider was aboard, let alone had access to her?"

"Another good point." Bess looked thoughtful. "What about the maid, Analyn? Maybe it was her, or the other cabin attendant. Either of them might have spotted Hazel while they were in there cleaning."

"Or what about the kid's parents?" George peered down toward where the family was now seated. "I mean, they seem like nice people, but so have a lot of the baddies you've busted, Nancy."

"I guess you're right. They certainly had access to the spider, since it was in their cabin." I chewed my lower lip. "But why? What's their motive?"

Just then Alan returned. "Sorry," he told Bess breathlessly. "They told me there's no time—show's about to start. Maybe we can get you a drink afterward?"

"Sure, no problem." Bess smiled and squeezed his

hand as he took his seat. "Thanks for trying."

As we waited, I thought about what George had said. Could Tobias's parents be in cahoots with their bratty son? Having a couple of adults involved made him a much more believable suspect. But why would they try to sabotage a ship? What could they possibly be trying to accomplish?

I was still pondering it when the show started. It was entertaining, but I couldn't seem to focus on it. About five or ten minutes in, I noticed that one other person didn't seem very involved in the show either. I saw Scott check his watch, then stand up and head toward the exit.

No big surprise there, I thought. *He's probably seen this show a million times.*

But his exit gave me an idea. "I'll be right back," I whispered to George, who was sitting beside me. "Bathroom break."

She just nodded, not taking her eyes off the action.

I made my way to the outside of the arena and glanced around, wondering where to start. The streets of Ketchikan were as crowded as ever, which wasn't going to make it easy to track down any of my suspects. If there was an Internet café in town, maybe I could check to see if Wendy was hanging out there. . . .

At that moment a knot of people moved aside, and I noticed Scott standing nearby. He was talking to a man I'd never seen before—his face wasn't one anyone could forget, given the large, jagged, ugly scar bisecting it. Scar Guy was maybe a few years older than Scott, dressed in ripped jeans and a grimy plaid flannel jacket. The two of them were leaning close together and appeared to be deep in conversation.

Then Scott quickly looked around, though he didn't notice me watching. He stuck one hand into the pocket of his windbreaker, pulled out something I couldn't see, and shoved it at Scar Guy. Scar Guy tucked whatever it was into his jacket, then took off without another word in the direction of the docks. Scott put both hands in his jeans pockets and started walking fast in the opposite direction.

What was that all about? I wondered. Something

about what I'd just witnessed had set all my sleuthing instincts on high alert, though I wasn't quite sure why.

I took a few steps after Scott, keeping him in sight, not certain what to do. Sure, Scar Guy looked kind of seedy. But so what? Scott could easily have friends or acquaintances in various ports, and I knew better than to judge someone on appearances. There could be a million perfectly innocent explanations for what I'd just seen. And Scott wasn't even on my radar as a suspect. Why waste time worrying about what he was doing?

But sometimes a girl just has to go with a hunch. Besides, it wasn't as if I had a better plan in mind. Putting on a burst of speed, I followed Scott as he rounded the corner and headed deeper into town.

CHAPTER TEN

Catch as Ketchikan

THIS IS A WASTE OF TIME, I THOUGHT AS I ducked into a doorway.

I'd already followed Scott for several blocks. Every so often he paused and glanced around, and I'd been careful to stay out of sight. It wasn't hard, since we were still in the touristy part of town and there were plenty of people around. Maybe if I was lucky I'd come across Wendy or one of my other suspects, and that would give me an excuse to give up this crazy idea of tailing Scott.

The crowd thinned out a little as we turned to head off the street and up a short walkway toward a low-slung wooden building. I hung back until Scott disappeared inside, then hurried forward. A sign by the door identified the place as the Totem Heritage Center.

"Cool," I murmured as I saw several intricately carved faces grinning or scowling down at me from a tall totem pole near the building.

But I wasn't here to sightsee. Pushing in through the door, I glanced around.

It took a moment for my eyes to adjust to the dim lighting. The place was small, making the collection of towering totem poles seem even taller as they loomed up in the center of the room.

There were a couple of older tourists wandering around, but I didn't see Scott anywhere. I wandered farther in, staring up at the poles. My footsteps echoed, seeming to bounce off the impassive totems. The place was cool, but a little creepy, too.

This is silly, I told myself. *I'm sure Scott's just here scoping out this place to include on future tours, or some other ship business like that. I should go, maybe try to track down Wendy or something.*

But I couldn't help remembering how Scott had acted as he walked here—stopping every few minutes to look back, as if he didn't want anyone to see where he was headed. If he was just going about his normal business, why would he act like that?

Besides, I was already here. I might as well follow through.

By now the tourists had disappeared into the adjoining gift shop. I glanced in there, but there was no sign of Scott, so I kept going, circling around the totems huddled at the center of the room.

Where'd he go? I wondered.

When I reached the back wall, I heard the sound of muffled voices. Spotting a door, I pushed it open, revealing the bright glare of daylight—and Scott's surprised face.

"You!" he blurted out harshly, freezing in place. "What are you doing here?"

My eyes darted from his face to his hand. It clutched a large wad of cash, which Scott appeared to be in the process of handing to another man. The second man was big and burly, with a wool cap pulled low over his broad, ruddy face.

"Gimme 'at," the man rumbled, grabbing the cash and then taking off, moving surprisingly quickly for someone his size.

"I—I—," I stammered, unnerved by the furious scowl on Scott's face. I looked around quickly, realizing we were alone in a small alleyway behind the building.

But when I looked back at him, his angry expression had melted away, replaced by a sheepish smile. "Sorry, Nancy," he said. "You startled me!"

"Sorry," I said, glancing in the direction where the other man had disappeared around the corner of the building.

Scott followed my gaze. "I guess you're wondering what that was all about," he said. "That guy's a poker buddy of mine—lives here in Ketchikan. I owed him some cash from the last time I was in town, and he called in the debt."

"Oh. Um, okay."

"I hope you won't say anything to the captain about

this." Scott bit his lip. "Ship employees aren't supposed to get involved with gambling while we're on duty, and I could lose my job if anyone finds out."

"Sure, don't worry. I won't breathe a word," I said, pretending to draw a zipper closed across my lips. But once I got back onboard, of course I was going to say something.

"Good." He was all smiles again. "Now, aren't you supposed to be at the lumberjack show? How'd you end up here, anyway?"

I babbled some excuse about needing air and going for a walk, which seemed to satisfy him. Then we headed out through the museum and parted ways outside.

As I hurried toward the lumberjack arena, I thought about what I'd just seen and heard. Scott's story made sense—he'd been sneaking around because he didn't want any of his coworkers to see him and possibly report him. And it wasn't as if he made a likely suspect for any of the trouble that had happened so far. I made a mental note to ask Becca what she knew about him, and maybe have George check him out online just in case. Otherwise, it seemed safe to forget the whole encounter. Well, I hoped it did anyway.

I arrived back at the arena just as the audience came pouring out onto the street. Almost everyone I saw was laughing and chattering with excitement, and I was kind of sorry I'd missed most of the show.

Then Alan spotted me and hurried over, with Bess and George trailing along behind him. "Where'd you disappear to?" he demanded. "That must've been one heck of a line at the ladies' room!"

I thought fast. "I always hate when people crawl back and forth to their seats during a show," I told him with a shrug and a smile. "So I decided to just hang out at the back and watch from there so I didn't disturb anyone."

"That makes sense," Bess said quickly, though Alan looked a bit dubious.

I couldn't really blame him. It wasn't really that kind of show.

For a moment I wondered if all this subterfuge was really worth it. Maybe I should just give in and tell Alan the truth after all. It would certainly be a lot easier than all this sneaking around, plus it would mean an extra set of eyes watching for clues.

"Anyone else hungry?" Bess asked cheerfully before I could decide.

"Starved." George checked her watch. "I vote we bag out of that fjord thing we have scheduled and find some food instead."

I glanced at Alan, expecting him to argue. But he nodded.

"I could go for that," he said. "Besides, I kind of want to get a better look at Creek Street. What do you say?"

Creek Street was one of the town attractions that we'd passed on our tour earlier. It wasn't exactly a street at all, at least not in the usual sense. Its colorful wooden buildings—shops, restaurants, historic houses, art galleries, and other attractions—lined a boardwalk-like pedestrian walkway set on tall pilings over Ketchikan Creek. We'd only caught a glimpse of it from the horse-drawn carriage, but our tour guide had recommended checking it out on foot later if we had time.

"Sure," I said. "Let's go."

Creek Street was even more crowded than the rest of town. Tons of people were crammed onto the antique wooden boardwalk, which I guessed had to hang a good fifteen or twenty feet above the water at this point.

Bess peered over the drop. "I hope these walkways are stronger than they look," she joked.

"Don't worry." Alan took her hand. "I'll keep you safe."

She fluttered her eyelashes at him. "Why, thank you, kind sir."

George groaned. "Is anyone else suddenly losing their appetite?"

"Funny." Bess stuck her tongue out at her cousin. Then she glanced around, her eyes lighting up when she spotted an Alaskan-themed gift shop just ahead. "Hey, as long as we're here, I should do some souvenir shopping. The people back home will be expecting lots of trinkets. Let's start in there!"

She made a beeline for the store's entrance without waiting for an answer. George was right behind her, but Alan paused to glance back at me.

"Coming, Nancy?" he asked.

"You guys go ahead. I'll hang here and people watch," I said. "Just tell Bess to grab me some souvenirs if she sees anything good."

I turned to gaze out over the railing as he headed after the others. Most of Creek Street was laid out on a gentle curve, following the creek's meandering course, and I had a pretty good view of the walkways farther along. I rested my elbows on the railing, enjoying the feel of the sun on my face, and idly watched for any sighting of Wendy, Tobias, or Baraz while my mind returned to the case.

Not that I had any new brainstorms. I felt as if we were going in circles, trying to match up suspects, motives, and most of all opportunity. What did anyone onboard have to gain? Sure, there was Wendy—it was possible that she was drumming up action and scandal so she could report it on her blog and attract more readers. But how did that motive fit in with the threat that had made Brock Walker cancel? She'd mentioned his absence in one of her blog entries, but only briefly.

Then there was Tobias. He definitely had a motive—he'd made no secret of the fact that he didn't want to be on the ship. And of course the tarantula incident almost had to be his doing, even if he wouldn't admit it. But I found it hard to believe he could have pulled off the pool incident so soon after arriving on the ship. And even if we threw his parents into the mix and assumed that they'd overheard me talking somehow, it seemed unlikely that any of them could have slipped that note into my suitcase. Or tampered with the heating and cooling systems on the lower decks, for that matter.

And what about Hiro? He'd been around for the mini-golf incident, and fairly close by when the "body" had been discovered in the pool. And I was pretty sure that I hadn't imagined that weird look Becca had given him. If we assumed the spider thing was a red herring, he might have been able to pull off just about everything else. But again, why?

Chewing my lower lip and squinting out at the sunlight glinting off the water, I tried to figure out if I was missing anything, overlooking any suspects. My mind flashed to Tatjana, who might have overheard me talking about the case. She was clearly several years older than Becca, but had mentioned reporting to her. Did she resent that? Could she be trying to make her up-and-coming young boss look bad, hoping to steal her job? Then I thought about Mr. Hawaiian Shirt, who always seemed to be hanging around behind the scenes and making cryptic comments. Could he have a motive we didn't know about?

But no matter how I tried to reorder everything, shuffling and reshuffling suspects, motives, and clues, I just couldn't put it all together in a way that made sense. All I knew was that *someone* was causing all sorts of trouble for the *Arctic Star*, and I needed to figure out who and why before someone really got hurt.

There was a sudden burst of activity behind me, and I glanced back just in time to see an ocean of red hair flooding my way. It was the family reunion group from the ship. The ABCs, who really did seem to know everything, had informed the table at dinner last night that the family's name was O'Malley, and that its members hailed from all over the country and even overseas and were more than two dozen strong. I smiled as I watched a four- or five-year-old girl with bright red pigtails race eagerly toward the gift shop where my friends had gone.

"Mary! Wait for me—you don't want to slip and fall in the water!" a woman shouted, hurrying after the little girl. She spotted me as she rushed past, and gave me a quick smile of recognition. "Oh, hello!"

"Hi," I said, though she was already gone. I squeezed back against the handrail, trying to stay out of the way as the rest of the group crowded past me, shouting and laughing and clearly having a ball.

Hearing a shriek from somewhere farther down the walkway, I glanced that way, hoping that little Mary hadn't gotten into trouble. I couldn't see her or her mother in the ever-shifting crowd, but just then I caught a sudden flurry of movement behind me, just at the corner of my eye.

"Hey!" I blurted out as I felt something slam into the backs of my knees. My legs buckled, my feet went out from under me, and I went flying backward. I scrabbled for a hold, but it was too late—I felt my lower back bounce off the stiff wood of the railing, and then there was nothing but air between me and the ice-cold water rushing along far below.

"Help!" I shrieked.

SPLASH!

CHAPTER ELEVEN

Putting the Pieces Together

AN HOUR LATER MY TEETH FINALLY STOPPED chattering.

"Are you sure you're all right?" Bess bent closer, peering anxiously into my face.

"I'll live," I assured her, running a hand over my damp hair. I glanced at Alan and smiled. "But it's a really good thing I had our own personal lifeguard around to save me. Thanks again, Alan."

My friends and I were back on the *Arctic Star*. I was lying on a pool chair on the lido deck, letting the warm sun bake off the last of the bone-shivering chill of my unscheduled dip in the creek. Who knew water could be so cold in the middle of summer? It was a reminder that we really were in Alaska.

"You're welcome." Alan shook his head. "I couldn't believe my eyes when I came out of that gift shop just in time to see you go flying over that railing!"

"Good thing you did." George grimaced, picking at a splinter on the lounge chair where she was sitting. "Bess was ready to stay in there and shop till we all dropped, so it would've been a while before we even noticed Nancy was missing. And with all those crazy reunion redheads running amuck, who knows if anyone would've heard her yelling from way down in the water?"

I shuddered as I realized, not for the first time over the past hour, how lucky I was not to be badly hurt— or worse. Fortunately, I'd landed in a deep spot in the creek instead of on a rock or something. And I'd managed to paddle over and cling to a piling while I waited for rescue, which had come quickly thanks to Alan's shouts for help.

I glanced around the pool area. It was deserted except for us—and occasionally Max, who kept hustling back and forth to fetch me more hot tea or dry towels. Alan had texted him as soon as we'd arrived back onboard, and the butler had appeared almost instantly. And I had George text Becca, telling her not to worry, that I was safe and sound.

I felt bad for pulling Max away from what was probably supposed to be a few hours off. I felt even worse for wishing I could get rid of Alan so I could discuss the case with Bess and George before the other passengers returned from their day in Ketchikan. Once again, I wondered if I should just bring him in on the secret.

"It's weird being practically the only ones onboard, isn't it?" Bess commented.

"Yeah." Shooting a furtive look at Alan, I decided to keep the secret. It was just too complicated to explain, and he wasn't the type of guy to accept a story like that without asking tons of questions. "Um, I just realized something—I really wanted to pick up a few postcards in Ketchikan. Think I've got time to run back to shore before the rest of the passengers come back?"

"Don't even think about it, Nancy! You need to rest after what you've just been through. Let me run out and get the postcards for you," Alan insisted—just as I'd hoped he would. "How many do you want?"

Moments later he'd disappeared in the direction of the exit. George grinned at me. "Nicely done," she said.

"Was I that obvious?"

Bess rolled her eyes. "I wish we could just tell him the truth. I feel bad keeping him in the dark and sneaking around behind his back."

"Me too, especially after what just happened," I admitted. "But come on, we can sit around feeling guilty later. Right now I want to find Becca. Maybe she'll actually have more than two seconds to talk while everyone's ashore."

My friends traded a look and a smile. "Even a twenty-foot fall into ice-cold Alaskan waters can't keep our favorite sleuth down for long," George quipped.

"Did you expect anything less?" Bess replied.

"Can I borrow your phone?" I asked George. "Mine's still drying out."

Soon I was texting Becca. Her response came quickly: MEET AT PROMENADE SNACK BAR.

"Good," George said, reading the message over my shoulder. "That lady who checked us back onto the ship said that's the only place serving food until everyone reboards later. And we never did get that snack in town, thanks to the diving detective here."

"Ha-ha, very funny." I quickly texted Becca back to say we were coming, then tossed George's phone back to her. "Let's go."

When we reached the promenade deck, Becca was standing outside the snack bar, shifting her weight from one foot to the other and looking anxious. As soon as she spotted us, she rushed forward.

"Nancy, I'm so sorry. Are you *sure* you're okay?" she asked, as she looked me up and down. Then she leaned in closer and said, "Something else happened."

"Wait—you meant there was *another* incident?" I said. "Did it happen onboard or in town?"

"Onboard, about an hour ago," Becca replied. "The big central chandelier in the main theater came down."

"Came down?" Bess's eyes widened with alarm. "You mean it fell? The whole thing?"

"Kaboom." Becca looked grim. "Luckily, the theater was empty when it happened, so nobody was hurt. But you could hear the crash through half the ship. Freaked out a few of the guests who stayed behind. Plus of course it made a huge mess—broken glass and wiring everywhere. The theater will have to stay closed until it's cleaned up, which means we're scrambling to move or reschedule all the events that were supposed to happen there soon, including Merk's big performance tonight."

"Whoa." I shook my head. "So much for my theory that whoever was causing all the trouble would probably go ashore today."

"Please tell me you're getting closer to figuring out who that person is." Becca's voice shook a little. "Because things seem to be escalating, and the guests are starting to notice."

I chewed my lip. "Well, most of our suspects were in Ketchikan today as far as we know." As I said it, I realized that I didn't really know for sure that Wendy had spent the day in town. I'd spotted her briefly on the dock when we'd disembarked but hadn't seen hide nor hair of her since. But I put that aside for the moment. "What can you tell me about Scott, the shore excursions guy?"

"Scott?" Becca looked surprised. "Is he a suspect?"

"News to me," Bess put in, raising an eyebrow.

I shrugged. "I caught him acting a little oddly when I stepped out during the lumberjack show," I told Bess and George. "I didn't get a chance to fill you in before my fall."

"I don't know him that well, but I know he's worked in the industry for a while," Becca said. "Captain Peterson himself recommended him for the job, actually. He's not your best suspect, is he?"

She sounded kind of unimpressed. Unfortunately, I was afraid the rest of the list wasn't going to change that. "Um, no," I said. "Like I said, I was just curious after seeing him today. We've actually been working a few other leads."

"Yeah." George snorted. "Like our eight-year-old supervillain."

"Huh?" Becca said.

"She means that kid Tobias," I said, feeling kind of foolish. "Uh, after what happened with his pet spider yesterday, we thought maybe he or his parents could be behind some of the other trouble. We're also watching Wendy Webster, that travel blogger with the weird glasses."

"I know who you mean. Hipster chick. Talks a lot." Becca nodded. "You really think she could be our culprit?"

"Maybe," I said. "We're also keeping an eye on one of the cameramen, Baraz. He keeps disappearing at odd times, and—what?"

Becca had started laughing. "You can cross Baraz off your list," she said. "I actually just found out why he kept disappearing, and it has nothing to do with sabotage."

"Really? What?" George asked.

"He's deathly seasick!" Becca announced. "Can you

believe it? Most people on a cruise ship don't even real-ize they're on the water. But apparently he's got such a killer case of motion sickness that he's been having to run off every few minutes to barf over the side of the ship! Poor guy had no idea until it was too late, and I guess for a while he thought he could power through it. But he just fessed up and will be leaving the crew for good here in Ketchikan. Marcelo just told me about it."

"Wow," I said slowly. For a moment I wondered—could Baraz's motion sickness be a cover story? Maybe he'd guessed that we were onto him and decided to take off before he got caught. "So when did he leave the ship?"

"Way before the chandelier came down, if that's what you're thinking." Her smile faded, and she sighed. "Baraz definitely isn't our bad guy. Whoever it is is still out there."

"Don't forget to ask her about that Hiro guy," Bess said.

"Oh, right! Thanks for the reminder." I glanced at Becca. Was it my imagination, or had she visibly started at the mention of Hiro's name? "So we've noticed that youth coordinator guy, Hiro, always seems to be around when there's trouble. How well do you know him?"

"Not that well. But I doubt it's him, either." Becca glanced at her watch. "Listen, I just remembered I'm supposed to track down the captain about something important. Talk later?"

"Sure, I guess. . . ." I let my voice trail off, since she was already rushing off down the promenade deck's broad central aisle.

"Wow, she was sure in a hurry all of a sudden," George commented.

I nodded, feeling uneasy. Was there something Becca wasn't telling me?

"Come on," Bess said. "Let's go in and grab something to eat while we decide what to do next."

We headed into the snack bar. There was a counter at one end where you could order sandwiches and other light fare. A dozen or so tables were scattered around a pleasant little courtyard with a fountain at the center.

At the moment the place was nearly deserted, though one table near the fountain was occupied.

"Check it out, look who's here," George said. She raised her voice. "Yo, honeymooners! What's up?"

Vince and Lacey glanced up and waved. "Come join us!" Lacey called.

We got our food and then headed over to their table, though I really would have preferred to sit by ourselves so we could continue our discussion of the case. Then again, what was there to discuss? Our suspect list was pathetic, the saboteur was getting bolder and more dangerous with every stunt, and I was all out of ideas.

"So you three are back early," Vince commented as we sat down. "Run out of things to do in Ketchikan?"

"Something like that," I said, not really in the mood to discuss my accident. "How has your day been onboard? Pretty quiet?"

"I wish!" Lacey's hazel eyes widened. "Did you hear about the chandelier?"

"Yeah, we heard." I picked at my sandwich. "Crazy,

huh? It's a brand-new ship, after all. You guys didn't see anything or anyone suspicious around the time it happened, did you?"

George shot me a look. I could almost see the thought balloon over her head: *Real subtle, detective!*

Luckily, Vince didn't seem to think the question was weird. "We spent practically all day holed up in the gym, so we haven't seen a soul except for the attendant." He chuckled. "It's always so crowded in there—we figured today was the perfect chance to not have to wait in line for our favorite machines, or share space in the sauna. It was great! Right, honey?"

"Yeah." Lacey still looked troubled. "Now I'm thinking we're lucky the elliptical machine didn't blow up or something. It's crazy how many things are going wrong on this ship. Maybe it really *is* cursed!"

"I'm sure it's all simply a series of unfortunate coincidences," Bess said in her most soothing tone. "It's just too bad it had to happen on your honeymoon."

"Definitely." Vince checked his watch. "Hey, sweetie, we'd better roll. Iris made us an appointment to get massages before the crowds return, remember? We don't want to be late."

"Okay." Lacey stood up and smiled wanly at us. "See you at dinner."

"Yeah." Vince slung an arm around her shoulders and grinned. "Don't let the ABCs eat all the rolls before we get there, okay?"

After they left, my friends and I sat there and finished our food. We also went back to talking, going over everything that had happened and all our possible suspects. But we still couldn't come to any new conclusions.

"It just doesn't fit," I mused, picking at my last few fries. "It's like there's a puzzle piece missing—some clue or connection we're not quite getting."

George shrugged and popped a pickle slice into her mouth. "Maybe we should bring the ABCs in as junior detectives," she joked. "I mean, they know everything there is to know about cruising, right? Maybe they could figure it out."

Bess sighed. "Or maybe we should just give up and

go get a massage too," she said. "That might help us think about all this more clearly."

I stared at her for a moment, then turned to look at George. "The ABCs . . . ," I murmured, my eyes going wide as that final puzzle piece finally clicked into place in my mind. "That's it!" I exclaimed.

"That's what?" Bess blinked at me. "You don't think the ABCs are the bad guys, do you?"

"No, but I think I just figured out who is, thanks to you two." I jumped to my feet, grabbing my leftovers and flinging them in the general direction of the trash bin. "I just want to check one thing to confirm it before I tell Becca. Come on!"

CHAPTER TWELVE

Busted!

"ARE YOU GOING TO TELL US WHAT YOU'RE thinking, or what?" George panted as she raced through the halls at my heels.

"Yeah, spill it, Nancy," Bess added.

In response, I just put on another burst of speed. "There's no time to explain," I tossed back over my shoulder. "If we hurry, we should be able to get this cleared up before the rest of the passengers come back."

I could hear George grumbling under her breath, but I ignored it. Soon enough we'd all know whether my new theory was right.

"Will you at least tell us where we're going?" Bess asked.

"The gym." We rounded another corner. "And here we are."

I skidded to a stop at the glass doors leading into the ship's state-of-the-art workout facility. Pushing through, I was greeted by the mingled scents of sweat and talcum powder. The lobby was all glass, steel, and dark wood. A bored-looking young man in a silver-piped tank top was perched behind a counter, reading a muscle magazine.

"Can I help you?" he asked, glancing up as we entered.

"Yes, I have a question for you." I did my best to sound normal, like an ordinary passenger with an ordinary question. "Some friends of ours were here working out today, and I just need to know—did they stay here the whole time, or did they leave for a while and then come back?"

"Friends of yours?" The attendant wrinkled his brow. "Who do you mean? The only person who's been in here all day is that guy." He jerked a thumb toward the large, open gym area off to the left.

Glancing over, I was surprised to see Mr. Hawaiian Shirt plodding along on one of the treadmills. That was kind of weird—he didn't exactly seem like the gym rat type.

But I wasn't too interested in that just then. My heart was pounding as I leaned forward. This was even better than I'd thought!

"Are you positive about that?" I asked the attendant. "Our friends Vince and Lacey weren't here a little earlier?"

"Nope." He shrugged. "Trust me, I've been sitting here all day."

I glanced at Bess and George, who both looked confused. "Vince and Lacey?" Bess murmured.

"Thanks," I told the attendant. Then I hustled my friends toward the exit. "Come on," I told them. "We've got to get over to the spa. And let me borrow a phone—I need to text Becca again."

George handed hers over as we rushed out of

the gym and back down the hall. "What's going on, Nancy?" she asked. "Do you really think Vince and Lacey are the ones we're after?"

I sent the text, then grinned at her as I returned her phone. "Yeah. And you guys were the ones who made me realize it," I said. "When Bess talked about how we should get a massage and then you mentioned the ABCs, it made me remember a couple of things I'd forgotten about until then. Like that one of the ladies thought she recognized Lacey from a Jubilee cruise they took once."

"I remember that," Bess said. "She said Lacey must have a sister who worked there."

"Only what if it wasn't Lacey's sister, or just her doppelgänger or whatever?" I said, jogging around a corner with my friends right behind me. "What if it was Lacey herself? The ABCs said the woman on the Jubilee cruise was her spitting image except for hair and eye color. And both those things are easily changed."

George gasped. "You mean you think Lacey worked for Jubilee?"

"That's my guess," I said. "And there's our motive. Lacey—and probably Vince, too—could be working undercover for Jubilee. What better way to sabotage their greatest competition? Especially since everything on the *Arctic Star* is totally state-of-the-art."

Bess and George still looked kind of confused, but there wasn't any more time to discuss it. We'd just rounded another corner into the hall where the spa was located. Becca was already there waiting for us, along with Captain Peterson and a pair of beefy uniformed security guards.

"Nancy!" Becca rushed forward to meet me. "What's this all about?"

Captain Peterson strode forward as well. "Yes, I don't understand what's going on here." His voice was stern, but his eyes looked anxious. I guessed all the trouble on his ship must be weighing on him even more than it was on Becca.

"I'll explain everything in a minute," I promised them both. "First we need to get in there."

I led the way into the spa. The front doors opened

into a large, luxurious waiting room. There was a table at one end where I guessed the receptionist normally sat, though it was deserted at the moment. One side wall featured a large mural of a peaceful ocean scene. The other wall was lined with shelves full of various spa-type products for sale.

When we entered, Lacey was kneeling in front of the shelves, holding one of those product bottles. The cap was off, and she was watching as Vince carefully poured something into the bottle from an unmarked flask.

"Hey!" one of the security guards blurted out. "What are you two doing?"

Vince and Lacey looked up, somewhat shocked. Vince recovered quickly.

"Oh!" he said with his usual easy smile. "Sorry, you startled us. Uh, we spilled some of this lotion here and were just trying to fix it. Sorry! We'll pay for it, of course."

"Yes you will." I stepped toward them, gesturing for the security guards to come forward as well. "Better grab that from him. The police will need it as evidence."

"Police?" Lacey exclaimed, jumping to her feet as the guard stepped toward her and plucked the bottle out of her hand. She grabbed for it, but it was too late. "We just said we'd pay—we didn't do anything wrong!"

Captain Peterson cleared his throat, looking confused. "Exactly what is going on here?" he asked me. "I can't have my passengers harassing one another, or—"

"These particular passengers are onboard under false pretenses," I broke in. "I'm pretty sure they're the ones who planted that fake body on the first day, and they were also responsible for the crashing chandelier earlier today. Among other things. Like tampering with the products in here—what'd you put in that lotion bottle, guys? Itching powder, permanent dye, or maybe something more deadly?"

The captain shot the pair a glance, a relieved expression flitting over his face. "Well, innocent until proven guilty and all that, but perhaps we'd better examine the bottle and its contents and see what we can find."

Vince and Lacey traded a glance. Their expressions had gone hard and wary—they clearly realized they were busted and there was no way they were going to talk their way out of it.

"We're not saying another word until we speak to a lawyer," Lacey said, her voice steely. So much for her sweet-and-sensitive act.

"We'll sue for wrongful arrest!" Vince sounded slightly hysterical. "Our lawyers will put you and the entire company out of business!"

"Yeah, that was your motive all along, wasn't it?" I turned toward Becca and the captain. "We're pretty sure they're working for Jubilee Cruises," I explained. "They came on this cruise to sabotage it—to do everything they could to cause negative publicity and press for Superstar. One cursed voyage is all it takes, right?"

"What?" the captain exclaimed.

"So how did you figure it out?" Becca asked me. "I didn't even realize that Lacey and Vince were suspects."

"They weren't until just now," I admitted. "But once I started thinking about it, I couldn't help but be suspicious that they were the ones who just happened to 'discover' that fake body in the pool, remember?

Lacey's scream was what attracted the attention of everyone within earshot, so lots of people would be sure to see it."

"That's right!" Bess exclaimed. "Then she stuck around to cry and shudder and tell everyone who'd listen how terrible it was."

Lacey glared at her, then at me. "You can't prove anything," she snapped.

I ignored her and explained to the captain and the others about the ABCs' comment at dinner the first night. "And there was one other clue that helped me put things together," I went on. "Something Bess said reminded me of it. See, when we ran into Vince and Lacey a little while ago, they said something about Iris scheduling a massage for them. That made me realize that Iris must be the maid assigned to their cabin."

"Iris?" George frowned. "You mean the same Iris we keep seeing in the hall outside our suite? I thought she was the maid for Tobias's cabin."

"No—Tobias's parents said she wasn't, remember?" Bess's eyes went wide. "Oh, now I get it!"

I smiled at her. "Yeah. That bugged me when they said it, but I forgot about it until the massage thing came up. Iris didn't have any reason to spend so much time in our hall—unless she was just snooping around the ship looking for trouble. When I found out she was Vince and Lacey's maid, I started to consider that maybe, just maybe, she was working undercover with them."

Captain Peterson turned to one of the guards. "Go find Iris and bring her to me," he ordered.

As the guard hurried off, I continued explaining. "I'm guessing Iris spotted that tarantula by chance the first time."

"Well, probably not chance exactly," George put in with a grimace. "I bet Tobias scared her with it on purpose."

"Whatever." I shrugged. "The point is, she must have told Vince and Lacey about it, and the three of them cooked up the idea to freak everyone out by planting it on the buffet. I'm guessing Iris sneaked into the cabin and stole the spider, and then one of the other two slipped it onto the buffet and just waited for the fireworks to start."

"Poor Hazel." Bess shook her head. "She could've been hurt or killed!"

George shot her a disbelieving look. "Are you seriously feeling sorry for a spider?"

"What can I say?" Bess shrugged. "I'm an animal lover."

I ignored them. "Once I figured out the first two big pranks—the spider one and the body in the pool— it wasn't hard to guess how they might have pulled off some of the other stuff. Iris could probably get access to the temperature controls, so that explains all the hot and cold cabins last night. Any of them could have started the rumors about the crew not getting paid, or sent Brock Walker that e-mail threat. And of course the happy honeymooners stayed onboard while almost everyone else was gone, so it would have been relatively easy for them to mess with the chandelier. Especially since we just confirmed that they weren't anywhere near the gym, where they claimed to be all day."

"Bad cover story, guys." George smirked at Vince and Lacey. "You should've just said you were in your cabin all day, or smooching on some deserted deck somewhere. You're supposed to be honeymooners—we would've believed it."

"Anyway," I continued, "we didn't see them near the mini-golf course, but it wasn't that crowded up there. Any of the three of them could've easily sneaked in there at some point and rigged that moose's antler to fall on someone."

"Yeah. Good thing Nancy has quick reflexes." Bess shuddered. "She could've been killed!"

"Wait a minute!" Vince blurted out, sounding panicky. "What moose? We didn't do that! And we weren't trying to *kill* anyone!"

"Shut up!" Lacey glared daggers at him.

But Vince didn't even seem to hear her. He shoved forward past the security guards. "No, seriously!" he told the captain. "I mean, okay, you caught us. I confess and all that—we're working for the vice president of Jubilee." He turned to look at Becca. "He hates your friend Verity, by the way. Says she's a traitor to the company. But he still likes your grandfather. That's why we sent you that message."

"Yeah," Lacey spat out. "Too bad you didn't listen."

"Wait, back up," I broke in. "What message? You mean that threatening e-mail Becca got before the cruise started?"

"What threatening e-mail?" Captain Peterson put in, sounding confused.

"It wasn't supposed to be a threat," Vince protested. "It was supposed to be a warning! We didn't want Becca to get mixed up in all this."

"More like you didn't want her to work for the competition at all," I said.

"Whatever." Vince shrugged. "My point is, yeah, we did most of that stuff, okay? But we never tried to actually hurt anyone, so whatever this moose thing is you're talking about, we had nothing to do with that! I swear!"

"Would you shut your big fat mouth?" Lacey snapped. "Or I'll shut it for you!"

"All right, I think I've heard enough." The captain gestured to the guards. "Take them into custody, and let's contact the local police."

A few minutes of chaos followed. Vince pleaded for mercy, while Lacey called him every bad name in the book. My friends and I stepped back and watched as the security guards hustled them both out of the spa. The captain followed, his cell phone pressed to his ear and Becca at his side.

"Think Vince was lying about the moose thing?" George wondered.

"Probably," Bess said. "I bet he panicked when he realized that could be seen as, like, attempted murder or something."

I shrugged, feeling troubled. "Maybe. On the other hand, those loose bolts might have been an oversight like we originally speculated." I bit my lip. "Anyway, I just realized something else. There's no way those two could've planted that note in my suitcase."

"But Iris probably could have," Bess pointed out.

"I guess. But why? She had no way of knowing I was

there to investigate, and otherwise it's just too random."

"Whatever," George said. "You solved the case, right? I mean, Vince just confessed right in front of us. So yay us—now we can relax and enjoy the rest of the cruise."

Just then Becca stuck her head back in through the spa door. "Are you three coming?" she asked. "The captain just called the Ketchikan police to let them know we're on our way. He wants you to come along and give your statements at the station."

"Coming," I said, doing my best to shake off the loose ends tickling my mind. George was right—we'd solved the case.

Yay us.

Later that afternoon I took back my ship ID as the check-in woman smiled and waved me through. "Welcome back aboard, Miss Drew," she said. "Just in the nick of time!"

I thanked her, though my words were lost in the blare of the ship's air horn announcing our imminent departure from Ketchikan. Bess and George had stopped to wait for me just past the check-in, though Becca and the captain had hurried on ahead.

"Well, that was fun," George said when I joined her and Bess. "When I heard we'd be going ashore at Ketchikan, I never thought I'd be spending so much time in the local police station."

"You and me both." I smiled. We'd spent the past two hours at the precinct, giving our statements and answering questions from the captain and the cops. Vince and Lacey had been arrested, along with Iris—it turned out my guess was right and she was a Jubilee plant too.

Bess stretched her arms over her head, looking happy. "So now that we're officially on vacation, what do you want to do first?" she asked. "Should we go get our nails done? Or maybe check out some of the shops?"

"Ugh." George made a face. "With all the activities they've got on this ship, *that's* what you want to do? Shopping and primping? You can do that stuff at home!"

"Before we do anything else, can we please get a snack?" I suggested. "Suddenly, I'm starving."

My friends agreed, and we headed for the stairwell. Halfway to the next floor, we heard the sound of voices somewhere just above us.

"Is that Becca I hear?" George commented. "She didn't get far."

When we reached the landing, Becca and the captain were standing there with Marcelo, Becca's boss. All three of them looked grim and anxious.

"What's wrong?" Bess asked.

Becca spun to face us. "I thought the trouble was over!" she cried. "But something else just happened— the ship's jewelry store just got robbed!"

"What?" George exclaimed.

"Are you sure that wasn't Vince and Lacey too?" I put in.

"Definitely not." Captain Peterson shook his head. "Marcelo says it happened within the past half hour or so—someone must have taken advantage of the usual pandemonium of the passengers reboarding."

By the way he was talking to me, I guessed that Becca must have filled him in on who I was and why I was onboard, though Marcelo looked confused. "We'd appreciate it if you didn't mention this to anyone until we've had a chance to look into it," he said, obviously still taking us for ordinary passengers.

"Of course," Bess told him.

"I'd better go look into this," the captain said, rubbing a hand over his face and looking weary. He glanced at Becca and Marcelo. "As you just said, we don't want this to get out to the passengers. So you two had better go do your thing and keep everyone happy—and distracted."

Becca and Marcelo nodded and dashed up the stairs to the lido deck, with the captain right behind them. My friends and I followed more slowly.

"Wow," Bess said. "What do you think of that?"

George shrugged. "It might not mean anything much," she pointed out. "I mean, jewelry stores get robbed all the time, right? Maybe someone sneaked onboard from the town or something."

I bit my lip as those nagging loose ends crowded back into my mind—that note in my suitcase. The moose incident. The heated argument I'd overheard in the kitchen. And even some of the pre-cruise mischief, which none of the culprits had fessed up to at the police station. Were those things just random red herrings?

"Maybe," I said slowly. "Or . . ."

I didn't finish. We'd just reached the deck, and I spotted Alan rushing toward us.

"There you are!" he exclaimed. "I was afraid you'd missed the departure." He shook his head mock sternly at me. "I still don't know why you all decided to come ashore to try to catch up with me. I told you I'd get your postcards, didn't I?"

Bess linked an arm through his. "We know," she told him sweetly. "But we remembered some other shopping we wanted to do. That's why I texted you to say we were coming back to town. It's just too bad we never found each other."

It was a pretty lame cover story for where we'd really been, but Alan didn't question it. As he started chattering eagerly about trying the ship's climbing wall or something, I traded a look with Bess and George, wishing we were free to continue our conversation.

But it didn't really matter, because I knew we were all thinking the same thing. There was no way that Vince, Lacey, and Iris had robbed the jewelry store—not if the timing was what Marcelo said it was.

Those loose ends started flapping away in my mind again as I realized that maybe we weren't going to be able to relax and enjoy this cruise just yet. . . .

Dear Diary,

OKAY, SO WE DIDN'T SOLVE *EVERY* mystery. But maybe on the next part of the tour— the train ride to Denali—I'll have time to think everything through, clue by clue, and help Becca.

Then I'll be able to pan for that gold!

READ WHAT HAPPENS IN THE NEXT MYSTERY

IN THE NANCY DREW DIARIES,

Strangers on a Train

"NANCY! DOWN HERE!"

I hurried down the last few steps to the landing and saw Becca Wright waving as she rushed up the next set of steps toward me. The cruise ship's atrium stairwell was deserted except for the two of us, just as she'd predicted. Almost everyone aboard the *Arctic Star* was gathered along the open-air decks watching the view as the ship chugged into the picturesque port of Skagway, Alaska.

"I don't have much time," I told Becca. "Alan thinks I'm in the ladies' room. He wants to get a photo of all of us at the rail when we dock."

"I don't have much time either." Becca checked her watch. As the *Arctic Star*'s assistant cruise director, she was always busy. "I'm supposed to be getting ready for disembarkation right now. But I just found out something I thought you'd want to know right away. The police caught the robber!"

I gasped, flashing back to the events of the day before yesterday. While the ship was docked in a town called Ketchikan, someone had robbed the shipboard jewelry store.

"Really, they caught someone already? That's amazing!" I exclaimed. "Who was it?"

"A guy named Troy Anderson," Becca replied, leaning down to pluck a stray bit of lint off the carpet. "I guess he's well known to the local authorities as a petty thief and general troublemaker type. They caught him over in Juneau trying to fence the stuff he stole."

I blinked, taking that in. It wasn't exactly the answer I'd been expecting. "So he wasn't a passenger or crew member on the *Arctic Star*?"

Becca raked a hand through her dark curls. "Nope.

Which is weird, right? I have no idea how he got onboard." She smiled weakly. "Maybe it's a good thing you're still here, Nancy. I hope you're in the mood for another mystery?"

The *Arctic Star* was the flagship of the brand-new Superstar Cruises, and this was its maiden voyage. However, things had gone wrong from the start. *Before* the start, actually. That was why Becca had called me. We'd known each other for years, and she knew I liked nothing better than investigating a tough mystery. She'd called me in—along with my two best friends, Bess Marvin and George Fayne—because she was worried that someone was trying to sabotage the new ship.

And she'd been right. Just a few days into the cruise, I'd nabbed the saboteurs, Vince and Lacey. They were working for a rival cruise line, trying to put Superstar out of business.

Then the jewelry store robbery happened—*after* Vince and Lacey were in custody. And I'd realized that maybe the mystery wasn't over after all.

"Do you think this Anderson guy had an accomplice on the ship?" I asked. "If so, maybe that person was also responsible for some of the other stuff that's been going wrong."

Becca bit her lip, looking anxious. "I hope not. Because I was really hoping all the trouble would be over after you busted Vince and Lacey."

I knew what she meant. I'd been trying to convince myself that the case was solved. That a few dangling loose ends didn't matter. That those loose ends were just red herrings, easily explained by bad luck, coincidence, whatever.

What kind of loose ends? Well, for instance, there was the threatening note I'd found in my suitcase the first day onboard. Vince and Lacey claimed to know nothing about that. They also denied being involved in most of the problems that had happened before the ship set sail. And they claimed to know nothing about the fake moose antler from the mini-golf course that had missed crushing me by inches. They also seemed clueless about the angry argument I'd overheard from the ship's kitchen that had ended in what sounded like a threat: *Drop it, John! Or I'll make sure you never make it to Anchorage.* And they insisted that neither of them was the person who'd pushed me off a raised walkway in Ketchikan, sending me tumbling twenty feet down into icy water.

I shivered, thinking back over the list. It didn't take an expert detective to realize that the most serious of those incidents seemed to be directed at yours truly.

"We have to accept that the case might not be over quite yet," I told Becca. "If the robber does have an accomplice on this ship, he or she might still try to cause more trouble. We'll have to keep our eyes open for clues."

"Do you think—," Becca began.

At that moment I heard a clang from the stairwell. I spun around and saw Alan standing on the top step of the flight coming up from below. He was staring up at Becca and me with a strange expression on his face.

"Alan!" I blurted out, cutting off the rest of Becca's comment. "I—uh—didn't hear you coming."

I hadn't seen Alan Thomas coming the first time I'd met him either. Had that really happened only a few short weeks ago? I'd been having lunch with Bess and George at one of our favorite cafés near River Heights University. Suddenly Alan had appeared beside our table, drooling over Bess and begging her to go out with him.

It wasn't the first time that type of thing had happened. But it was the first time Bess had said yes. She said it was because she saw something different in Alan. He was different, all right. He was outgoing and cheerful and kind of excitable—nerdy, as George liked to call it. I guess that worked for Bess, because the two of them had been together ever since.

Then Becca had called, begging me and my friends to come solve her mystery. Our cover story was that we'd won the cruise in a contest. When Alan found out we would be staying in a luxury four-bedroom cabin, he'd practically begged to come along. He was an environmental studies major at the university, and this trip was supposed to give him a head start on his sophomore year research project. That was nice for him, but it made things kind of complicated for the rest of us. See, Becca had sworn us to secrecy—we weren't supposed to tell a soul why we were really onboard the *Arctic Star*. Not even Alan. Had I just blown our cover?

"Nancy! I've been looking all over for you!" Alan exclaimed, hurrying toward me. "Did you get lost on the way to the bathroom or something? You're missing some amazing views."

"Nope, I was just chatting with Becca, that's all." I forced a smile, studying Alan's face. Had he overheard what Becca and I were talking about? His gray eyes looked as guileless as ever. Or did they? Something about the way they were peering into mine made me wonder just how much he'd heard while coming up the stairs. . . .

New mystery. New suspense. New danger.

Nancy Drew
DIARIES™

BY CAROLYN KEENE

NANCYDREW.COM
EBOOK EDITIONS ALSO AVAILABLE
From Aladdin | simonandschuster.com/kids